Other Books in the Vintage Library
of Contemporary World Literature

Aké: The Years of Childhood BY WOLE SOYINKA

Correction BY THOMAS BERHNARD

Maíra BY DARCY RIBEIRO

Masks BY FUMIKO ENCHI

The Questionnaire BY JIŘÍ GRUŠA

ONE DAY OF LIFE

ONE DAY OF LIFE

MANLIO ARGUETA

TRANSLATED FROM THE SPANISH

BY BILL BROW

AVENTURA

The Vintage Library of Contemporary
World Literature

VINTAGE BOOKS

A DIVISION OF RANDOM HOUSE

NEW YORK

An Aventura Original, September 1983

Translation Copyright © 1983 by Bill Brow

All rights reserved under International and
Pan-American Copyright Conventions.
Published in the United States by Random
House, Inc., New York, and simultaneously in
Canada by Random House of Canada Limited,
Toronto. Originally published in El Salvador
as *Un Día en la Vida* by UCA Editores, San Salvador.
Copyright © 1980 by Manlio Argueta.

Library of Congress Cataloging in Publication Data

Argueta, Manlio, 1936-

One day of life.

Translation of: Un día en la vida.

I. Title.

PQ7539.2.A68D513   1983   863   83-48032

ISBN 0-394-72216-7

Manufactured in the United States of America

The translator wishes to acknowledge the
assistance of Don Daso.

ONE DAY OF LIFE

5:30 A.M.

Not a God-given day goes by when I'm not up by five. Already when the cock has crowed several times, I'm up. When the sky is still dark and is pierced only by the shriek of a bird, I'm alert.

The *clarinero* flies over our hut, saying clarinero-clarinero. I don't need anyone to wake me up; it's just that the *clarinero* is an early riser, loud and disturbing.

In any case, I alone decide when it's time to get up. I have a trick to be punctual: the cracks between the sticks that make up the wall. The sticks of my hut are of *tihuilote*; it's a tree that's common around here, and it gives big sticks. The only problem is that they're brittle, and you always have to keep replacing them. We like *tihuilote* because it doesn't attract termites. Termites eat wood, and before you know it, everything is ruined.

I peek at the night through the cracks in the wall.

After lying for so long in the same spot, we become attached to spaces, to a stain left by the dung of a bull, to a little figure on the straw roof. What I like most is to watch the sky as the night disappears. An everyday event. I can see the morning star through a little hole. I know it because it's so big. It flickers, on and off, on and off. At first I can't see it; then it arrives at the little hole as the stars and the moon and the sun walk across the sky.

When the big star gets to the little hole (I know exactly where it is), it's four in the morning, and by then I'm awake but I don't get up; I lie there pretending to be asleep, snuggling up to José if it's cold or lying with my backside to him if it's hot. And through the cracks in the wall I can see the pictures of the sky: the scorpion, the plow, Santa Lucía's eyes and all the others.

The bird that flies overhead is the *clarinero*; I know it because it heralds itself: clarinero-clarinero. And as dawn approaches you can see the ever-changing colors of its feathers.

The *clarinero* glows.

They say it behaves like the dead because it spends so much time near cemeteries.

I like to watch it flying and singing. Dawn is nothing but a flock of birds: among them the *clarinero* is supreme because of its chilling blackness.

The sky turns the color of the blood of a dead bird.

Where the hill begins to rise, the dawn's first rays appear. The color of a firebrand in the night. A burst of sparks that makes me say: How beautiful! As beautiful as the Virgin's mantle. Then the sky becomes as clear as well water at high noon. Little bits of colored glass. Chips from a broken bottle. And clouds floating under water. Clouds are the blankets of God. The sky is a Guatemalan weave of many colors. This is part of life. This is something I remember from when I was little, maybe eight or ten, I don't remember. That's when I met José. The sticks of the hut's walls have changed, but not the spaces, the cracks in the wall. Nor has the morning star that peeks in as it goes by. Nor have I.

Doña Rubenia, Lupe is already getting pretty on you. And from behind the cupboard I looked at my breasts, which stuck out like the beaks of *clarineros*. He knew me when I was just an innocent little girl. *Say good morning to Don José; don't be silly, go on. Has the cat got your tongue?* Ever since then, when I wake up, I'm already thinking about José, as I stare at the darkness that frightens me. And I feel so happy at dawn—it is as if the leaves of the trees were aflame. I'm very happy; it's true, I've never been sad. But please don't talk to me about the darkness and the night because they make me piss on myself. *I've been thinking: if you give me Lupe you won't have to worry; she can help me, I'm tired of being alone.* And I got embarrassed as I was entering and heard "Give me Lupe." *Girl, get out; can't you see that grownups are talking?* I ran into the passageway, but I could still hear a few words. *I know she's still a kid but that's exactly why I like her, because at her age she's nice and proper and I'm going to be worthy of her.*

My eyes contain reflections of the Guatemalan weave. If I look to the sky, my eyes become full of sparks, like lights that shoot from the feathers of roosters. Skyscapes of bloody wounds. Skyscapes of bloody wounds. A wound is a wound.

I begin to tremble—it's the coldness of the night that refuses to die. The memory of Justino, perhaps.

It's the same coldness of *tamarindo* leaves, trembling, dewy. One knows when it's the coldness of death; it comes from another place, it comes with a certain fear, or as if one were no longer of this world. Teeth chatter, click-click-click, goose bumps, chills, hair standing on end. The never-ending shakes.

Holy Mother of Jesus, conceived without sin.

That's the only way to regain courage and endure—well, we're not going to keep trembling out of cowardice. Back then you used to wake up first. You would get up and go to the mango tree to piss, and I would hear the sound of the machete as you unsheathed it and wiped the blade with the palm of your hand moist with spit. Perhaps it was my family's influence that made me somewhat cowardly, because I was raised only with brothers and they were always scaring me: controlling me, looking after me, and telling me to be careful, not to go that way, not to walk in the dark; you know all the pampering you get if you're a girl (and even more if you're the only girl). I couldn't even look at caterpillars. Just the thought of seeing one scared me, those with tiny horns on their heads and little green tufts; I wouldn't even look at banana plants at night. *Siguanabas* and *Cipitios* are painted on the banana leaves. Dawn is a very happy time for me because I like light so much, and I like it even more when the sun rises out of the bush at six in the morning; light rises like a kite over the mountains.

Good morning.

With the Lord I go to sleep, with the Lord I awake to the blessings of God and the Holy Spirit.

I put on my semi-mournful skirt; this is how I've dressed ever since my mother died. I especially like the kind with little flowers and dots against a white background—any design so long as it's black because that's what I promised my mother when she was dying. I have only three dresses, but semi-mournful clothes don't show up that much the filth of pigs that is splashed on you, especially around feeding time, when the pigs crowd in on you. You might not believe this, but pigs are the most gluttonous animals I know.

When I get up, I go straight to the well; I draw ten buckets of water—for bathing, for pig feed and corn, and to water some plants in the yard. Chepe and Justino planted them.

We were lucky to find water almost at the surface of the earth; we're the only ones around here who have a well. Most people have to go to the river or the brook—they prefer not to spend money for digging a well. We wouldn't have had one had José not found the water. He noticed how that little patch of earth was always wet, with the lemongrass tree green year round.

Lupe, there's water here, I know what I'm talking about. I thought his discovery was pointless since we couldn't afford a well digger.

Here in Chalate it isn't necessary to have water in the house, since there's so much river water, and if you don't want to go to the river you can go to the brook. So you won't have to worry about going so far to fetch water. One has to walk more than half a mile to reach the river. The brook is closer but sometimes it is dirty, especially when it rains a lot and there's the danger of flash floods. *You know what you need to do to pay a well digger.* But José dug the well himself. The water was right on top; that's why the lemon tree stayed green. *The pigs will love it, José, because they'll have enough water so they won't die in the summer heat.*

And as far as water is concerned, another thing I always have is lard soap. The soap is sacred like corn: not only does it kill lice and eliminate dandruff, but it keeps hair soft as silk and you wear out fewer combs because they go through the hair easier. *On Sunday I'll help you bring water from the brook.* And we used to pour it into a big earthenware jar which we had buried near the fireplace. Now I'm the one who draws water from the well; it's simple because the water comes up with only four tugs of the rope. You don't have to kill yourself to get ten bucketfuls.

This is man's work, he'd say when I returned from the river with the water jug on my back. That's why we're so lucky to find water so easily. *And you were the one who didn't want to dig a well.* It wasn't that I didn't want to.

Suddenly the *clarinero* bird flies overhead, making cuio-cuio. It describes a black line in the golden sky, because it's almost five-thirty, and that's when the stars in the firmament all say goodbye, and only the roundest and largest ones remain.

I always cross myself in the presence of the morning star. With the Lord I go to sleep, with the Lord I awake. You do it by habit. I don't know why, but when sunlight begins to fade, I start to get anxious; it just takes hold of me, all of a sudden, this sense of desperation. Maybe it's the magnetism of the day gathering force like a stream of red water.

Hurry up with the coffee, 'cause already it's getting late.

The chickens have already jumped down from their perch and are begging for corn. They come close and begin to pick at the ground, eating pebbles and bits of eggshell.

The chicks puff up their craws. It's a cacophony in the dawn with its rosy sky.

Inside, the children jump out of bed calling, "Mama, Mama." And everyone remembering you because at this hour you are waking them up with a few swats on their rear ends.

Then they're up and about, with machetes, ready to go to the coffee plantation.

"Hurry up—the chickens are already jumping down from their perch," goes a peasant song. "We're going, Mama." And they put on the pretty hats José gave them for Christmas.

Coffee and hot salted tortillas for breakfast.

This is our life; we don't know any other. That's why they say we're happy. I don't know. In any event, that word "happy" doesn't say anything to me. I don't even know what it really means. After what happened to my son Justino, I prefer to stay closed up inside myself. It's not that I get sad. It's something I can't explain.

Sometimes we have a good time, that's true. There's no reason for my people to suffer my pain with me, though we've always known how to share equally the good and the bad.

I go from plant to plant, watering the little chili peppers,

9

watering the lime tree and some seedlings of *guisquil* and *pipian* and a *zapote* tree that sprouted on its own. Next I prepare mash for the pigs, which from the moment they get up won't leave me alone, following me and banging into my shins. I throw a few kicks their way so they'll let me prepare their food in peace. *You know, Lupe, these pigs are a lot of grief and the money we get for them doesn't even cover their feed.* The pigs have been our savings for gifts for the children at Christmas. That's why I always keep a little herd, so even though they're a lot of work, we always make a little something selling them to Don Sebastián, who makes tamales. And as they stomp around they dig holes everywhere and leave the patio full of turds and *nigua* bugs. *But, Lupe, you keep being stubborn as ever.* And I won't even tell you how they get in the house to see how much damage they can do. These pigs sure are enough to drive you crazy, but they're our only little hope for when the children ask for something that we can't deny them—at least once a year one has to buy them a new shirt or pants for a special occasion. Everyone wears new clothes at Christmas and the children expect to get something from baby Jesus. *Leave that to me. I'm the one who's supposed to provide for them, and even if I have to struggle, I'll get them something, be it only one of those clay whistles you buy for kids.* The only toys we buy for them are whistles—they're cheap and the kids have a lot of fun with them. They go around blowing them all the blessed day, tweet-tweet.

If you think the pigs are good for something, then that's up to you. It is my business. In November I'll sell them at a good price.

Part of the money is for sweets and the rest is for note-books, pencils and textbooks for those going to school. I buy a change of clothes for the older ones so they can get dressed up on Sundays like real people; they aren't babies anymore and I can't have them walking around in rags, especially because now they're earning a few cents and they give me all their money.

Once the pigs have eaten their corn mash, they go to the mudhole near the well and begin to grunt. But that's in the afternoon, because in the morning all you have to do is throw them an ear of corn once in a while and they'll be satisfied.

Sometimes, at high noon, I'll go shopping at the Detour: for salt, coffee or some treat like canned coconut or preserves, which the kids like, especially when they return in the afternoon tired from doing chores at the farm.

The only thing we don't need to buy is corn, because we grow enough for a year and have even a few pounds left over to sell to the neighbors.

The Detour is a half a kilometer from our place. Don Sebastián's store is there; he gives us credit, and his prices aren't high compared to those in town. Once a month José goes to town to buy those few little necessities that Don Sebastián doesn't sell—lime for cooking corn, some kind of medicine for stomachaches or whatever is necessary or is better to buy there. Before leaving I will have put the beans on the fire and drawn more water from the well for use during the rest of the day.

I do all this while the youngest children are at school and the older ones are at work with their father in the fields. The kind of work available at this time of the summer is preparing the ground for sowing, because the rainy season is approaching. Before, the fields were not cleared with machetes—it was enough to set fire to them. But then some people from the city came and said that it was better to clear the fields by hand because fire ruined the lands, and now even though it's more expensive, the owners prefer that the thickets and weeds be destroyed only with machetes. It's better for us, too—we get a little more income. By this time of the year all harvesting is over and the only work that one can find is clearing the fields. And it works out well since the coffee plantation is only a few miles away and the owner pays well, José has told me. I would like all our children to learn to read so that they won't have to live as hired hands and suffer as much as we have. Especially since we don't have anything else to give them to do in the off-season, when we earn hardly enough for beans or maybe a shirt for Holy Week. The children are our only hope—at least they may give us a hand in our old age. When you're old, you're a bother and don't have enough strength to work. There's nothing to do but die. If you have children, they'll always turn out good and somehow manage to help the old folks.

I agree that we should sacrifice and send the little ones to school, so they won't be ignorant and so no one will cheat them. The truth is we can barely scrawl our signatures on our IDs so as not to appear illiterate. Do you know how to read? Yes. To write? Yes. But we only know how to read letter by letter and perhaps not even that well, because it's been years since I've seen a printed page, and the letters I see are on signs or labels in the store at the Detour that I know by heart, though every now and then I glance at the numbers and doodles traced by the children when they're doing their homework. As for José, I doubt if he even knows what the vowels are. I haven't asked him if he's forgotten how to read. He doesn't need it. Only his machete and his friends. That's his life.

My parents could send me only to the first grade. Not because they didn't want to but because we were so many at home and I was the only girl, in charge of grinding corn and cooking it and then taking tortillas to my brothers in the cornfields.

My brothers used to kill themselves chopping and hoeing. My father, too.

My mother and I would take care of the house. All together there were fourteen of us—I and my folks and eleven brothers—even after three children had died. They died of dehydration. I remember how my father held the last one by his feet so that blood would run to his head, but nothing happened. He died with his head caved in. All their heads sunk in after serious bouts of diarrhea; once diarrhea begins there's no salvation. They all died before their first birthday.

Children die of dehydration only when they're very little, since their bones are very soft, and if you're not careful, they get diarrhea and the forehead sinks in.

Children go to heaven. That's what the priest used to say. And we never worried. We always believed that.

Our only concern was that they might die suddenly, without having been baptized. Then it would really be bad because children have original sin. If they die with original sin, they go directly to purgatory. Purgatory is not a place where one suffers much, but it's still a site of punishment;

13

there are always flames even though they don't burn much.

That's what the priests told us when they came on their missions. So as soon as we see children with a little diarrhea, we rush to have some holy water sprinkled on them. And look for their godfather.

5:45 A. M.

One day I was going to throw a stone at a frog. It was then that I first heard the voice of conscience.

I raised my hand. I had just turned twelve. I remember the time because I had become a woman—I got my first period.

I was about to throw the stone, when I heard the voice of conscience, a voice that told me not to throw the stone at the frog. "What is the poor thing doing to you?"

I was petrified. That's how I became aware of that voice that comes from within. The voice is not ours. I felt a little afraid. And I associated the voice with punishment.

"Don't you see it's a sin?" it said. The stone fell behind me, almost hitting me on the neck, and went down my dress. Hearing the voice, I stood with my hand raised, holding the stone, and I had to let it go as my fingers were loosening their grip.

That voice lives within us. It talks to us even in our sleep. It always watches over us.

That's why when we're asleep, we sob, sob in the most genuine of ways.

The voice of conscience is a dream. Put better, it's not a dream; it only resembles one. In dreams we see things through rose-colored glasses, but the voice of conscience is severe, absolutely unpleasant. It is a voice for scolding: don't do that—do this. Don't do it because it's a sin. The loss of freedom, then.

And when the stone fell behind me, the frog took off hopping, jumping, splash—into a green puddle of water. His great leap frightened me.

"If you stone the frog," the voice of conscience told me, "he will squirt milk on you, and your skin will dry up. Your skin will become like the frog's, wrinkled and ugly." Well, the voice of conscience does us favors, but they're favors that no one asked for.

One good thing that happened to me with the voice of conscience was when it took the form of the *Cadejos*. I was coming from the Detour, having bought some rolls of twine. And because I'd stopped to talk, I was late and darkness fell. We had to restring the bed because the cords had broken. "Go buy them, you, I'm too tired." That's what José told me. "You'll have to hurry before it gets too late." And I grabbed my shawl and ran off to the Detour. "Oh, Don Sebas, night has caught up with me today." And to make matters worse, there wasn't any twine in the store. "Lupe, wait. Take this candle and return it to me tomorrow. Don't be silly and break a leg in the dark."

And I asked him how many candles he had, and whether he'd be left without light. "It doesn't matter. We're going

to bed anyway." "Ay, Don Sebas, you're like a mother hen."
I said thanks and took off. "In any event, the candle will
only go out."

It would have been better had I left earlier, but I struck
up a conversation with Don Sebas's wife, and it got real
late. "Okay, don't take the candle if you don't want to, but
don't go around saying that I was stingy with light." And I
started to run. "See you later, Niña Concha." "God be with
you," she yelled when I'd reached the road.

I thought there wouldn't be any problem once I got used
to the darkness. "Hope a devil doesn't jump out at you,"
Niña Concha yells at me. "Devils come out when it's light
or dark," I manage to yell back.

And because I'm thinking about being afraid, my knees
began to knock.

I walk on the rabbit-foot grass, stepping on the soft grass
so as not to fall into a hole; where there's rabbit grass, there
are no holes.

And all of a sudden I see a big animal standing before
me. And the big animal tells me not to walk on the grass.
I recognized in his voice the voice of conscience. But I
thought it was the *Cadejos*, by its fragrance of orange
blossoms, because the *Cadejos* likes to lie beneath orange
trees and the fragrance clings to it. "Well, what does this
dog want?" I said to embolden myself. I knew it wasn't a
dog. And I wasn't a bit afraid. Well, it was the Good
Cadejos because instead of scaring people he gives them
a kind of confidence. They say that when the Bad *Cadejos*
comes out, he makes you feel like pissing, by just looking
at you, never mind about talking.

"Move over," he said.

And I moved over, away from the little path of rabbit

grass. And then he disappeared. After taking only a few steps along the dirt road I felt the first strike of the rattlesnake. Luckily I got out of the way in time and it couldn't get me. I heard it rattling near me. "I've got to get away," I said, and ran like mad. It wanted to come at me again, but I heard only its noise because I was far away. "Fucking snake," I said.

The voice of conscience saved me from the rattlesnake. What's more, that voice illuminated my way. Because it knows everything. That's why I say the voice of conscience belongs to one and doesn't belong to one. It comes from only God knows where.

6 A.M.

We're from Chalatenango. From the outskirts of Chalate, a place about ten blocks from town. That's why we call it the Kilometer. The people here like to sing. And laugh over nothing. Almost all of us are poor but we don't consider it a disgrace. Nor something to be proud of. It never mattered to us because for many years life has been the same. No major changes. We all know each other and treat each other as equals. Someone who owns a cart is considered the equal of someone who owns nothing more than a machete.

José plays his guitar and sings *rancheras*, popular political songs that are enough to drive you crazy, or love songs; "Look how I yearn for your love" is his favorite. Or maybe he knows that one best.

We like the *rancheras* because they have pretty lyrics that everyone can understand. It's only been a little while since another kind of song; it was when the boys arrived at church, accompanying the priest. They sang so-called protest songs.

Yes, but lately everything has changed.

Once upon a time the priests would come and hold Mass in the Detour's chapel, giving us hope: "Hang on just a little longer." They'd tell us not to worry, that heaven was ours, that on earth we should live humbly but that in the kingdom of heaven we would be happy. That we shouldn't care about worldly things. And when we'd tell the priests that our children were dying from worms, they'd recommend resignation or claim we hadn't given them their yearly purge. But despite any purges we gave them, they'd die. So many worms eat the children from within and have to be expelled through their noses and mouths. The priest would tell us to be patient, to say our prayers and to bring our little offerings, when we took our children to him, when we brought the skeletons with eyes. One of my children died on me that way—from dehydration and from being eaten up by worms. Fortunately, we lost only one to that disease.

—Well, what's the matter with your baby?

—Ay, look dear Father. All of a sudden he began to poopoo water and more water.

—Maybe the milk you gave him was bad.

—No, Father, he never drinks milk.

—Well?

—It's worms, Father.

—You need quickly to give him a purge and then feed him properly. What are you giving him to eat?

—During the day he has a little drink made from corn flour, and at night sugar water.

—And how old is your baby, Lupe?

—Nine months old already, Father.

—You ought to at least give him cheese; if you don't have milk, cheese is a good substitute.

—In the store at the Detour you can buy some milk, which is the same thing, but we can't afford such luxuries. Besides, José's boss has told him, and we know so already, that milk gives children bellyaches and that it isn't good to get them used to drinking milk or eating meat.

—Did the landowner tell you that?

—Yes, and it's something everyone knows.

—Well, what is there to do? May God's will be done.

—It would be good of you to sprinkle him with holy water, Father.

—But, my dear child, you forgot to bring his godfather.

—Tomorrow there'll be plenty of time to find him, Father. I thought you could recommend some medicine; you see, I would have wanted to give him a purge made from the *altamiza* plant, but I'd have to go to the gully for it and José isn't here.

—My dear child, I'd go get the *altamiza* for you, but I know it isn't going to cure him. In cases like this only worm medicine helps.

—And where can we get the medicine, Father?

—That's your business, my child. But why don't you bring his godfather tomorrow and we'll baptize the baby, just in case . . .

And the priest would tell me to keep the faith, and that if the child were not saved, it would be because of someone's carelessness. Faith in the Church cannot be lost. And

21

that Christ had died this way, and that the priest would sprinkle holy water on him so that he'd go straight to heaven without having to pass through purgatory.

We couldn't do anything, only accept; it was God's will. Sometimes we didn't even cry over our children because we convinced ourselves that death was a prize God had given them. It was better to die than to suffer in this vale of tears.

Well, the priest had so enthralled us that even our hearts were turning to stone. I didn't even cry for my son when he died, because death had become so natural that we thanked God for taking him away—persuaded by what the priest who'd come every two weeks to our part of Chalate would say to comfort us.

—It's a good thing you brought it because this child is very ill.

—Yes, Father, please sprinkle water on him.

—Of course, that's why we're here—to save the souls of sinners. You should have brought him sooner. The child is more dead than alive; you've delayed a great deal in bringing him. Imagine if he'd died on the way.

—It's because two weeks ago when you were last here, he was well and healthy, and I never thought he'd be sick so suddenly.

—Still, you people always leave everything until the last minute.

—I even had his godfather ready, Father.

—Well, wait over there. I'll take care of you in a minute, after I say Mass. The child will last for a little while longer.

—Thank you, Father.

Then all of a sudden the priests began to change. They

started getting us into cooperatives. To help each other, to share profits. It's wonderful to help someone, to live in peace with everyone, to get to know each other, to wake up before sunrise and go to work with the children, herding pigs and selling eggs for a good price. We'd take the eggs to town instead of to Don Sebas' store because he pays next to nothing; he never fails to be a skinflint in this regard. Everything around here was getting better. They also changed the sermons and stopped saying Mass in a jargon that nobody understood; we no longer had to hear about *Dominus obispos*, which we used to make fun of, saying "*Dominus obispu*, I'll kick the ass in you." Now Mass is a serious affair, ever since the priests began to open our eyes and ears. One of them would always repeat to us: "To get to heaven, first we must struggle to create a paradise on earth." We began to understand that it was better this way. And we would ask them why the priests before them forced us to conform. "Forget the previous ones," these younger priests would say.

What's important is that our children don't die. To let a child die is the worst sin one can commit. At the first sign of illness we'd look for the priest; they used to be in Chalate more often. We started being less afraid of priests. Previously they used to instill fear in us; we believed they were like magicians who could annihilate us with the simplest gesture. Besides, we didn't trust them. They would speak in hoarse voices, as if from other worlds or from the profundities of God. It seemed as if they walked on air, from here to there, in their long black robes. They'd ask us for a few pounds of corn and some chickens. We couldn't say no because we considered it a sin to deny anything to a priest of the Church.

—Father, I'm fattening a nice little hen for you to have during Holy Week, if it pleases you.

—Thanks, Lupe, though it's better not to offer anything until you have it.

—I'm telling you so that you can start making preparations.

—No, no, that's not the way to do it; either bring me the chicken next time or forget the whole thing. Don't you know that Holy Week is four months away?

—Then I'll bring you a little pig for Christmas.

—Look, woman, what am I going to do with a pig if I can't keep it at the parish? The chicken is fine because you can give it to me all seasoned.

—Well, Father, I'll bring you the meat of the pig ready to roast.

—That's more like it, that's something else. But don't deprive yourself of meat by giving it to me.

—No, father. I'll keep the feet and the head and the intestines and the blood to make sausage.

—It's up to you, my dear; you are not obliged to give me anything.

—Of course, Father, the pleasure is ours.

—Tell José to feed the pigs generously so they'll flesh out a bit, because Christmas is only three weeks away.

The presence of a priest, with all his seeming saintliness, produced nothing but fear and suspicion in us. They were meaner than a rattlesnake (and may God keep you from provoking their wrath or hatred), they'd smoothly retaliate by threatening you with hell. Of course, when they wanted to be nice, they were nice.

—Look, Lupe, tell José if he doesn't come to Mass, not to come around later for absolution.

—He's working.

—On Sunday?

—Yes, Father. Since the picking season has begun, he wants to take advantage of every minute, now that there's work.

—Then he's not at home?

—No, Father. He went down to Santa Tecla and he returns every two weeks.

—And you stay by yourselves?

—Yes, except in January, when the kids can help pick coffee that has fallen to the ground. I go, too. It's a chance to earn a few cents more.

—Well, Lupe, give this candy to the kids, but don't let them eat all at once; give them one at a time. That way maybe they'll last until Christmas.

—Thanks so much, Father.

—And don't forget to bring Chepe. Tell him to come to Mass, to stop being such a freethinker.

—Yes, Father.

After a congress was held I don't know where, as we were told by the young priests who began coming to Chalate and who visited our own house, religion was no longer the same. The priests arrived in work pants and we saw that, like us, they were people of flesh and blood— only better dressed and their voices were normal and they didn't go around asking for chickens, but on the contrary they would give us little keepsakes from the city—here's something for your little boy—when they came to our place.

They'd descend to the Kilometer and would come to see how we were living. The previous priests never got as far as where we lived—they took care of everything in the chapel; they'd get out of their jeeps there—and then after Mass they'd get back into them and disappear in the dust from the road.

To be sure, these new, friendly priests also traveled in jeeps, but they would come to the Detour and visit us: how are you doing? How many children do you have? How much are you earning? And we didn't understand their way of talking, the words they used. They even formed the first cooperatives and we made a little profit. They taught us to manage money and how to get a good price for our eggs, chickens or pigs.

We used to know how to do that—we weren't dumb; but since we never had any surplus, we had no money to manage. The only money we ever saw went right past us; no sooner had we earned a few cents than they were spent on aspirin, rubbing alcohol for cholic, bismuth compound for diarrhea, medicinal powders for *maldeorín*—those kinds of things. Now at the end of the year we have something left over for toys: a car, a plastic ball or marbles. In sum, what could I tell them. "This is so they won't go around slack-jawed, Lupe, when the other children get real toys. It isn't throwing money away to buy them those luxuries. On the contrary, they will divert themselves and won't wander off, running the risk of being bitten by snakes."

Well, back then something happened that had never happened before: the Guard started appearing in our neighborhood, and when we saw them we'd spread the word and have to watch out, because the Guard is very strict; you can't walk around, for example, with a machete strapped to your wrist because for sure you'd get an ass-whipping or would be fined more than any poor person could ever pay.

The Guard would say that it wasn't necessary to carry machetes around all the time; but since men are accustomed not to part with their machetes, it's hard to convince them

that when they're not working it's unnecessary to carry
them. They feel abandoned without their machetes; it's a
necessary companion. The thing is, sometimes there are
mishaps, especially on Sundays when they drink too much
rum. That's why the Guard is so severe and doesn't fool
around when it comes to taking a machete away from even
the toughest guy with a few good kicks in the ass. "If you
walk around with your machete tied to your wrist, we're
going to chop off your hand." And they mean business.
Well, that's one thing about the Guard: they always keep
their word. Whoever messes with them knows what he's
in for; the Guard has always maintained law and order, by
beating up or shooting those who don't obey the law. Rarely
has the Guard killed anyone around here, even though
whenever someone turns up dead one knows it could have
been the Guard. Besides, the people around here have
always been peaceful; they're not troublemakers, they're
not even heavy drinkers. Sure, they relax with a few drinks,
but they don't go crazy. Even Chepe himself has a couple
of drinks from time to time, but he knows he can't spend
money because we've got so many mouths to feed. I haven't
had any trouble with him that way.

—Where are you going with that machete, Chepe?
—To cut firewood . . .
—Be careful and don't let the Guard see you.
—It doesn't look as if they're coming this way today . . .
—Don't let them see you, because today is Sunday.
—They won't see me, Lupe. I've given them the slip
  several times already, because I can smell them coming
  from a mile away.
—Don't forget, there's a first time for everything.
  And they began telling us that the priests had made us

insolent, had filled our heads with strange ideas. And now
it wasn't enough for them to ask to see our identification if
we were carrying a machete: they wanted to know if we
were going to Mass. What did the priests tell us at Mass?
And at first we didn't understand anything. For what
reason should we recount every detail? Guardsmen could
go to Mass and find out for themselves with their own ears.

It was only to frighten us so that we'd back away from
the Church. "Yes, we're going to Mass and you should see
how good this priest is, Officer, he isn't like the others." And
were those sons of bitches here and those sons of bitches
there, faggots in robes, giving us religious instruction for
the purpose of disobeying them? And they'd point the barrels
of their guns at us, and we'd better stay away from the
chapel, and even on Sunday when we were going to the
Detour, they were hiding in the undergrowth and would
suddenly jump out and ask for our personal documents
and where we were walking to, and whether we were going
to hear Mass. To go see the priests, these sons of bitches
wear fancy clothes, even white shirts; for that they have
money but not to feed their kids. We wouldn't pay them
any mind. We knew them all too well: they get angry, but
if we remain quiet they don't do anything more than insult
us. Just to frighten us away from the chapel. And then
they go around saying that the landowners don't pay them
well. And would there be any Communist singers at church
this Sunday. And we who knew nothing. We went because
we were practicing Roman Catholics. The truth is that
Chepe and I weren't very devout, but it was a pretty place
to go on Sunday and we liked what the priest would say—we
felt we were learning something. "I think these assholes from
around here are homosexual. I wonder how many whores

the priest has screwed. Maybe because he's such an exotic
and gallant type, they've fallen in love with him." And words
to this effect, while the men take documents out of their
shirt pockets to prove that they live around here. "Or perhaps you've all seen the priest take a piss." Guffaws, even
though at heart they were furious. When a guardsman
laughs at you, you'd better be ready to get kicked in the
ass. We'd be real quiet, obedient and quick to show them
our papers. And no one could afford not to have papers,
God forbid! It's enough to make you want to bust up
these pussy cowards. Their hatred of the priests they'd
take out on us. They wouldn't dare touch a priest because deep down they were afraid of them. Like us, the
guardsmen have been Catholics, and almost all of them are
peasants; what happens is that they've gotten education and
we haven't. They've had schooling, you know, because to
be a guardsman requires training. What makes them
haughty and strong is that they've studied to be authorities
so that the law will be obeyed. The law has always been
hard. They say that only by being that way can they force
you to obey the law; there are people who won't be good
otherwise. We're only interested in being bad, they say. I
don't know, I've never done anything bad to anyone, not to
José or to my children. Evil appears suddenly. Where it's
least expected. They defend private property—that principle is sacred—because it is possible for our hands to be
stained with blood; but to appropriate what isn't ours, that's
out of the question. We're as pure as the driven snow. So
things are put.

The guardsmen were afraid of the priests because they
wouldn't stay quiet: they scolded them. Why did they go
around doing mean things along the roads? They weren't

getting paid to give people a hard time. It went in one ear and out the other. A few days later they'd be up to their old tricks again, treating people badly. One day they dared the worst. Something that made us feel like dying: the priest was found half dead on the road to the Kilometer. They had disfigured his face, had brutalized him all over. Someone was passing that way and saw a naked man moaning in a ditch. They'd stuck a stick up his anus and it was there still. The priest's voice could barely be heard. A little farther up the road, his robe was hanging all ripped. When they came to tell us, we all went together. Right there we lifted him on to the road to wait for a vehicle that would take him. And there I realized we had become hardened, because no one grieved or cried—only "poor thing" said within and in anguish because he was a priest; something had happened that we had never imagined. It was a nightmare. We realized that saints could descend from heaven. After that, nothing shocked us; all that remained was for it to rain fire and for cats to chase dogs. They found the priest's jeep farther up the road, burned, in another ditch. As if it had ignited itself. That's all we needed in this life. From that moment on, any sin was going to seem petty.

6:10 A.M.

We had never gotten anything from the Church. Only given. Little things, it's true. It simply taught us resignation. But we never came to think that priests were responsible for our situation. If one of our children died, we would assume the priest would save him in the other life. Most likely our dead children are in heaven. At least we were consoled.

Always chubby and rosy-cheeked.

We didn't wonder whether they were happy. Life on the outside didn't matter to us. Nor did the life of a priest.

If they offered heaven to our children, we didn't think they were fooling us.

And when they changed, we also began to change. It was nicer that way. Knowing that something called rights existed. The right to health care, to food and to schooling for our children.

If it hadn't been for the priests, we wouldn't have found out about those things that are in our interest. They opened our eyes, nothing more. Later we were on our own. We had to rely on our own resources.

We learned to look out for ourselves. The young priest who had been wounded in the anus didn't come back. Later we learned that he'd gone abroad because he had received threats on his life. For us things were good; for others they were bad. Especially for the landowners, who are the ones who suffered most when we demanded our rights. They spend more and earn less.

Besides, once we learned about the existence of rights we also learned not to bow our heads when the bosses scolds us.

We learned to look them in the face.

We grew a little in stature, because when you bow your head you become smaller and if you raise your head high your spirit also rises. Months passed and new young priests came and said the same things. Our eyes were opened even more. And José, who had once been pious, easily became friends with the priests. "We've got to join cooperatives, they'll help us out." One's hopes are green, but sometimes they mature. And how are we going to join if we don't have anything? And he would say, even if it has to be with the pigs. We have to be better about raising chickens, every egg laid must be hatched, and forget about eating the little pigs, let them grow. That's how we came to have four dozen chickens and more eggs to sell to the cooperative.

Sometimes people would come from the city to sing at the church, songs about poverty. Learning that the truth is something else. We were deceived. One should be good. Kindness should not be confused with submission.

And thinking about the young priest who had almost been killed.

If they do that to priests, without any regard for the

Church, what would they do to us? It was better not to go out after quitting time, especially to the Detour, because it was so far away and because guardsmen hung around there until after seven o'clock at night, when the last bus left for Chalatenango.

And forget about having a few drinks after hours. You know how José liked to have his little taste of rum, and the poor man used to suffer from not being able to chat a while with his friends at the Detour.

Business began to fall off for Don Sebastián since his clientele had diminished. Don Sebastián would send them home because it was time to close up shop.

For two whole weeks no guardsmen were seen at the Kilometer.

As if they knew what they'd done.

Later they were back again. At first they started around Don Sebastián. "Have any of those sons of bitches come to say Mass at the chapel?" Don Sebastián would string them along. He had no other choice. Even though his prices are high, he'll always side with the poor. Imagine, ever since what happened to Father Luna they've stayed away; there's the chapel, completely dirty, no one will even come close to it. Especially since they know that he was our neighbor and we're united. And since they didn't believe him. They would have wanted him to take the bait. "And you, who do you think fucked that Commie priest in the ass?" Don Sebastián goes behind the counter to throw away the bottle caps from the soda pop they'd bought from him. No one ever found out who did it. And the guardsmen pestering him, trying to trick him to see if he'd slip up. "Those who shoved the stick up the priest's ass must be pretty fiendish fellows." And he pretending to yawn, because he doesn't

have any more bottle caps to throw away behind the counter
and he has to face their provocation head on. That's possible. Enjoying the ginger ale bubbles . . . "What's the
matter, cat got your tongue?" He laughs because there's
nothing else he can do. "I've had a toothache all morning."
They invite him to have a beer and he tells them that he
doesn't drink when he's on the job. If we invite you. "In
such cases one has to play dumb," Don Sebastián told Chepe.
"It's not on account of the expense, but as the owner of the
store it's not in my interest to drink because there go all my
profits; that's why even if they invite me, I won't accept.
Of course, if I showed any signs of nervousness, they'd notice that I was putting them on, and that would be the end
of Sebastián. With you I can have a little taste, but with
those people I couldn't because they'd expect me to take
them into my confidence."

José told me all of this soon thereafter. "Just imagine,
Lupe, how far their cynicism goes."

"They abuse honorable people," I said to José.

And at another time, while visiting the store:

—I don't know whether Chepe told you.

—He said something.

—They say that communism is going around filling people's
heads with ideas and that Father Luna was nothing but a
Red.

—So one isn't suppose to even think.

—They say that what's bad are Communist ideas, mixing
politics and religion.

—And what is that about, politics and communism, Don
Sebastián?

—Saying that one ought to enjoy life on earth so as not to
have the right to go to heaven.

"That's what the guardsmen resent most, Lupe, because in a subtle way the priests stick it to the landowners and they know the priests are the ones who encouraged the people to protest. The guardsmen maintain that the priests have been won over by the Red demon and that the blame lies with one of those Roman popes and that in time they poisoned him; otherwise all Catholics would be Communists." "Well," I said, "there once was a time when the priests only offered us heaven and it didn't matter to them that our children were dying or whether the medical clinic was good, or whether we even had one, it was all the same to them."

—And to think that previously the priests never left their houses on the plantation; they used to spend all their time there, and they only came out when it was time to give Mass.

—That's what I say, Lupe. I'm not defending the guardsmen. What's happening is that the priests have gone to the other extreme and don't want to have anything to do with the customs of the Church. They ought to be neutral; that way nothing would happen to them.

—It's just that Christianity says to do good deeds for the poor.

—And that's why the landowners have gotten on them. Nowadays they can't stand the sight of them—you see, the priests have betrayed those who have always treated them well.

—Don Sebastián, why are you taking the Guard's side?

—No, look, Lupe, I'm only telling you what they tell me when they come here to drink ginger ale. You know I'm friendly with them only because I have to be.

"I understand," I say. What I still don't understand is

why the guardsmen side with the rich. Ticha's son, for example, is a guardsman, and we all know the misery she undergoes to feed herself and the grandchildren that her daughters left her when they went to the capital to better themselves.

One understands these things, it's true; one knows. What's difficult is to know how to explain them. Don Sebastián also knows. Maybe even Ticha herself; the poor woman goes around in rags because, you see, everything she and her husband earn goes for beans and corn for all the kids. There are five grandchildren.

José also understands, and sometimes he knows how to explain things with words.

MARIA ROMELIA

*Well, yes, I was one of those who went down to the Bank
to get an answer concerning a cheaper price for insecticides
and fertilizer, but the Bank was closed. We staged a little
demonstration. Then someone yelled at us to run. And we
ran, you'd better believe, we ran. Well, eight radio patrol
cars were coming after us. They started shooting and they
hit me—a bullet made a shallow wound in my left arm. Then
we arrived at the place where the buses were parked, but
they weren't there; the police had driven them away. And
we didn't know our way around San Salvador. I was with
my cousin Arturo; I stayed close to him because he is, or
was, smart for a fifteen-year-old. And he told me that we
should go to the nearby church, the San Jacinto church, I
believe. But the police had already occupied the church in
case we had any intentions of seeking refuge there. At that
moment we saw a number 38 bus, and my cousin yelled:
"Look, it says Chalate." And we ran toward the bus. By*

accident we'd come across the line that goes through our region. So I told him let's get on. And there were other passengers, other companions. Then, as we began to move, we noticed a helicopter following us. When the bus would stop, so would the helicopter. We could see it well from the windows. Then a girl began letting groups of us off at each stop. And the helicopter would hover. And the girl would let another group off. Arturo and I were next, that's what the girl said. Then we spotted a patrol car following us. We arrived at a police checkpoint. Of course, they told us to get off, said they were going to search us. So, once we'd gotten off we put our hands on the bus and spread our legs; but they didn't search us. They started shooting. And we crawled under the bus. They fired under the bus. And I felt the bullets whizzing by. Amid the gunfire we got back on the bus. When all of us were on, they closed the door and killed the man who was driving the bus. They had all gotten on the bus. Only one policeman remained outside near the door, aiming his machine gun at us. By then we were all lying down in the bus. And the police told us that at the slightest movement we'd all die. Then they shot at the windows to break them, and the pieces and splinters of glass fell on us. I remember that my cousin Arturo didn't move; I thought he was dead. And then, yes, they shot my right hand. Blood spurted from it. Then they stopped shooting. I told the girl in charge that they'd messed up my hand. And that we should get off the bus. And so, in front of the police, I stood up and got off together with the girl. Maybe because we were kids they didn't shoot. When we left the bus, we saw the radio patrol car behind us. And the federal police told the radio patrol car to call for another helicopter. That they wanted another helicopter. And from the heli-

*copter hovering above us they started to fire. Then I saw
other men hidden in ditches, lying on the ground and aiming
at the bus. As soon as we were out we stopped to look. Then
we asked a policeman for some money, because we'd lost
the purse and we had to take another bus. And the policeman gave us some change. "And you, kid, did they hurt your
hand?" he asked me. "You got off without a scratch," he
said to the girl who had been letting off groups at a time
and to whom I clung. "How old are you?" he asked.
"Thirteen," she tells him. At that moment another policeman grabbed the girl by her hair and took her back to the
bus. A little while after, he and two other policemen grabbed
her by the waist and heaved her into the bus through one
of the broken windows. I myself stood by watching. And
what luck she had, she wasn't hurt by broken glass. Well,
soon she was outside the bus again and I saw her throw
herself into a ditch. Right then I saw the policemen throw
bombs into the bus. Tear gas canisters.*

*And a huge cloud of smoke started coming out. And
then they threw another bomb in and the bus began to
burn with the people still inside, because throughout all
this the men had had to lie on the floor of the bus because
if they had left, they would have been killed. Then, after
they threw the tear gas, the policemen went back into the
bus to have a look. And then they started shooting at the
people. I could hear them screaming. And then the bus was
destroyed. Then I ran toward the ditch where the girl had
gone. And I shouted at her from the bushes but she didn't
answer. I walked out near an irrigation canal and I jumped
into it.*

*Nearby there was a house and I headed toward it. By
then more than an hour had passed. There was a little gray-*

haired lady who spoke to me, "Girl, what happened to you?" because my dress was drenched with blood. And there was another child inside, she told me. And to my surprise it was the girl from the bus who was sleeping on some burlap bags. "Don't wake her up because she had to cry herself to sleep," she told me. "If you want, you can take off your dress and put on this old thing while I wash the blood out of it." And I wrapped myself in the Guatemalan blanket and threw myself on the burlap bags. I had slept only a little while when I was awakened by the voice of an old man talking to the old woman. And then I heard the old man saying that they had been digging some ditches nearby when two helicopters started shooting at the number 38 bus near the Apopa exit and that the bus had caught fire and that they were cutting open people's ribs so that they'd burn better and they were giving them Christian burials in the ditches.

And the next day the girl told me she was going to leave me at the hospital because I had an ugly wound. And that I would not be able to get home the way I was, that I could even lose my hand. And I told her, "You go, then." Because I'd come to trust her as if she had been my mother. And she took me to the hospital and said goodbye. Before that I had asked her what village she was from but she didn't want to tell me. Then I asked her only about my cousin Arturo, if she remembered him, and she said they'd found the corpse of a boy about fifteen years old. A brother of mine who had also gone to the Bank passed by later in another bus and saw the burning of number 38 and thought about me; but no one wanted to get off and look. And my family looked everywhere for us—which seemed an impossible task at first—until they found me in the hospital.

You see, they asked my brother if he had seen Arturo and me. And he said no, because he went separately in another group and it seemed that those in my group had gotten lost and that the bus had left us; and that probably we were coming on the regular 38 route. And my mother was very upset. Until they found me.

I took ten days to heal, and if they didn't come from home it was because all the hospitals were being watched to see if relatives come to look for those who were wounded. After eight days they dared to approach the hospital. Only they never found my cousin, either dead or alive. Once she'd been reassured, my mother took me home. "Ay, child," she said to me as she walked over to my bed. "Ay, my child, see how we must suffer because of so much poverty, think about how hard we work and still can't make ends meet even to eat, to buy beans, let alone clothes." And I tell her, "Don't worry, Mother, if we struggle, we'll get something; at least they'll give us seeds to sow, or fertilizers for these fields to yield a good crop." And she tells me, "I wonder what the cost of the sacrifice will be. I don't believe they're going to give us anything—that's an illusion. If we don't work, we don't eat." And I tell her, "It's not a matter of begging, but of claiming our rights, because the government has said that the Bank is supposed to make loans so one can buy seeds and fertilizer." And she says to me, "Look how young you are, not even thirteen years old, and you have to go around risking your life; it would have been better had I gone to that demonstration in San Salvador. For all intents and purposes one is already old. It doesn't much matter if they hit us with a bullet. But you haven't yet seen much of life. You still have a right to be in this world; the way I look at it, that's the only right we should ask of the government: to

41

*be able to live in this world. We must have been born for
a reason." And I say, "You're exaggerating, Mother."
And she says angrily, "Exaggerating! How am I exaggerating when we don't even know if you will lose your hand."
And I tell her, "Don't worry, it was just a scrape, and if
the hospital let me go it's because I'm out of danger." And
she tells me, "Imagine if you were to lose your hand—the
only thing that enables you not to suffer from hunger, to
work. What would you do without your right hand?"*

*That's how mother gets pessimistic. She's been like that
ever since they took my father away. He had gone to live in
Ilobasco to look for work—there's a lot of work cutting
pineapples there and the pay is good. My father is always
away from home; he follows work—where there's work he's
there. We almost never see him because he's off earning
enough for food. Because we all work just for food. We live
off miracles. Sometimes he comes home every two weeks.
The last time he told us he'd be away for a month, when he
went to cut pineapple: "Behave yourselves and help your
mother," he said. "I'm going to see if I can bring you a
piece of cloth to make a dress out of," he told me. He'd
never been away for so long before. They say the Guard
took him away because he had organized a group of farmworkers in San Salvador. I didn't see him. There were so
many people that I didn't see him.*

*My father is organizing the Christian federation. He told
me that even though I was young I could belong to the
federation so that I'd begin to have my wits about me.
I joined but I didn't attend the meetings often enough—
you see, I help my mother take care of the children, my
brothers and sisters. She goes to the big house to work,
to do washing and ironing. Since there's no one to take*

care of my brothers and sisters, I do the housework, I
see to everything. That's why when people from the Christian federation come to invite me I don't always accept,
because Sunday is when my mother has to work the hardest.
Sometimes good friends say we're going to take all of you,
so that you'll be able to go out at least; they take good care
of the children. That's how I've been able to attend the
meetings, with the children. Sometimes they make a ruckus:
they cry and cry. And I feel I'm too much trouble for my
friends. I tell them to leave me behind. It's just that
children get very sleepy easily and that's what makes them
cry. And they tell me to put them to sleep on the ground.
And they spread a piece of burlap for them to lie on. They
must have worms to cry so much. So that's why I'm famous
for attending meetings with three children.

One of my little brothers is only eight months old, which
is to say he's still a baby; the other is two years old; only
the little girl doesn't give trouble. She's five, and she helps
me at least by carrying the bag. And I tell my mother, 'It's
good that you and Father are alive because if it weren't for
you, keeping house would be impossible." We chat about
these things while she applies a hot compress of guarumo
leaves. On my wounded hand. There we were near what they
call the door. And my mother says, "They're looking for
you, Maria Romelia." "Let them in," I say. And I see it's the
girl from the demonstration. The one who let groups of us
off the bus at a time. And I say to her, "What are you doing
around these parts?" And she says to me, "I was visiting my
grandmother and she told me there was someone wounded
around here, with a bullet wound in her hand, so I thought
it was you." And I say to her, "And you who were so good,
maybe I wouldn't be here if it hadn't been for you." And

*she says to me, "Oh, no, you had great presence of mind
to get off that bus the way you did." And I tell her, "You
won't believe how much trouble has come our way." But
I'd better not continue. I'll only say that my cousin Arturo,
well, we've given him up for dead. "The poor boy," she
says. And I who didn't even know her name. So I ask
her, "And what's your name?" She has brought me some
little oranges to make me a refreshment. Some animal
crackers. "My name is Adolfina; I'm Guadalupe Fuentes's
granddaughter." And my mother asks her, "Whose child
are you?" My friend answers her, "I'm María Pía's child."
I offer her an animal cracker. "Oh, no, how can I take any
from you when I could only bring that one little packet,"
she says. And she continues talking: "My grandmother
had given me that packet of crackers, but when it occurred
to me that you might be the girl who was with me in the
bus, I thought I would bring them to you, and then I
picked these oranges from the tree at my grandmother's
house; they were the last ones." And my mother tells her,
"We've all suffered a little, if it's not one thing it's another.
Look at what happened to your Uncle Justino," my mother
continues saying. "They hate us especially because we've
opened our eyes," says Adolfina. "Your grandparents suffered a lot," I tell her. "The one who suffers most is Mama
Lupe," she says. "She has to be alone—Papa Chepe sleeps
in the hills ever since they threatened him," she continues
saying. "It's a calamity what's happening in the region;
we're being left without men," my mother says. "You
mustn't be frightened," says Adolfina. "That's right," I say,
taking courage from the words of my friend. "Someday our
misfortunes will end," my mother says. "We women are
being left alone. They want to finish off all the men. Imagine,*

José, as good as he is, sleeps in the hills." "And your father, does he also sleep in the hills?" Adolfina asks me. "No, the Guard took him away and won't say where they are keeping him; he's disappeared," I answer her. "And what's your father's name?" she asks me. "Emilio Ramírez," I answer. "I've heard talk about him," she says. "What can you tell us about him?" my mother asks. "He was captured near Ilobasco with my father, soon after I arrived at my grandmother's place." "We're fed up with asking about him. They insult us, they make fun of us but good, all that we must suffer," says my mother; she pauses and then continues, "So you are María Pía's daughter? You almost never come around these parts to see your grandmother because I would have seen you. And your mother never returned to the Kilometer." "With the children it's been hard for her to come around here; only I can make it every once in a while," says my friend. And she continues, "When I was a little girl, they would bring me here for months at a time, above all because my parents used to go to Santa Tecla for the coffee harvest every year and my grandmother took care of me. You could say that she raised me; you should see how much I miss her when I can't visit her." "Maybe I saw you once at Don Sebastián's, but we never spoke," I tell Adolfina. "Yes, I remember you. What happened was that you were smaller, but even though you've grown you have the same face," says Adolfina. And so on. "And to think that you came upon each other in such difficult circumstances during that business on the bus; luckily you escaped, but my nephew Arturo must have come to an end there. They didn't even return his body. My brother couldn't pray for him on the ninth day. If you're a relative you keep hoping that someday they'll turn up around here. Maybe they'll feel sorry for our human pain

45

and let them go, if they're still alive," that's how my mother talks, always complaining and full of hope, the poor woman.

And on and on. "I think that maybe the end of the world is coming, so much evil can only have that as an explanation, imagine, well, look what they did to your Uncle Justino, what a barbarity, and to think that Lupe is so courageous, they say she didn't even cry, I always admired your grandmother's strength, she's one of a kind, because what can you do but endure and endure and believe that at least someday you'll have some tranquillity that you're going to live in peace and your children will have enough to eat"—you can't stop her when she gets emotional, and if you contradict her she gets upset. We listen to her attentively. Poor Mama, I think, while tears come to the eyes of my friend. Suddenly Adolfina seizes a moment of silence: "I know you're in the Christian federation. It is the way: we must organize ourselves so they won't be able to abuse us. I'm in league with the farmworkers." After a little while we start talking about my hand instead. "Thank God she got out of the hospital all right," says my mother. Adolfina leaves a little later. When I see her leaving, I get a lump in my throat.

6:30 A.M.

I'm happy today. Chepe stayed home last night to sleep. He left around five in the morning. Maybe that's why I woke up thinking about things.

Snuggling up to him as I was, hugging him. The warmth of José. Being next to him without talking, close to him, to the sweat of his shirt, my face against it, the way one does with small children, his wet shirt, the humidity that clings to clothes after a hard day's work.

He appeared in the backyard yesterday afternoon among the banana plants. Pijiriche was sniffing around restlessly, and the next thing you know he took off toward the back of the yard.

—Pijiriche, leave the hens alone . . .

And he doesn't pay me any attention, wagging his tail as if lamenting. And I yell at him again:

—Take care not to scare the hens . . .

And I see him jump for joy, his affectionate plaintive sounds. Because that's how he is: he even pisses from happiness when he sees Chepe.

He came out like a ghost.

—But, José, you could have thrown even a pebble to warn me that you were nearby. Such a scare you gave me!

And he tells me he wanted to give me a surprise—just imagine appearing all of a sudden behind the house. He has done it many times, but on this occasion he frightened me because I wasn't expecting him. Usually José doesn't come home to sleep; he goes to the hills, like almost all the men from our region. And I also don't see him during the day because he's working. From the mountains he goes to work. After Justino's death they came to threaten him, and if he didn't want to depart from this world, he'd better leave home.

What was the poor man to do? They convinced him. That's right; well, you see, the thing is that he didn't want to go, he wanted to remain with the rest of the people because already all the men were going into the hills. They convinced him. So did I. "Do it for your children," I told him. "The three little ones we have." "Well, I'll go," he told me.

And as he didn't look convinced, I told him, "Don't worry about us, we know how to take care of ourselves, and if you aren't here, I don't think they will bother us."

But José only hemmed and hawed, which is to say he was not entirely convinced. "You could go today after work; that way I won't be waiting for you." "All right," he said. And since he can't bear not seeing his children, he came on Sunday for the whole day. "There's no danger during the day," he tells me. And it's true. Those people are like bats; they attack only at night. "We sleep under a *guanacaste* tree; after clearing away the brush and cutting the grass, we each pick out our little spot," he tells me.

He goes to the hills without wanting to, I know. "That's how we're going to have to get along until this crisis passes. Luckily the children sleep like a rock; they don't wake me up at night, as you know," and he listens to me attentively.

It's cold without him, that's for sure. But I have my blanket of many colors. José gave it to me for Christmas. "I brought you this," he said. And we almost had a party we were so happy. Well, you see, at night it gets very cold, even though the hut is fortified with sticks. In the daytime it gets so hot, especially in the summer.

At the first crack of dawn he knocks on my door. The children are still asleep. He has his coffee and two hot tortillas with beans. And then he goes to work; he barely gets to see the children because at that hour they still aren't awake.

Last night he did come to sleep. Taking his precautions, he appeared in the backyard. Pijiriche first discovered him. And I thought the dog was playing with the chickens.

I almost didn't sleep, it's true. By four o'clock I was already looking at the sky. I wondered what time it was. Looking at the morning star. Twinkling signs at me through the sticks. I was also winking back.

Looking at the morning star brings good luck. The star that announces the time to put the corn on the fire. And looking directly at it is best. When it goes up and down, as if it were going on and off, it gives good luck. Ah, if that were true, I'd always be lucky. I love to look at it; there isn't a God-given day that I don't wake up to greet it.

49

José says that I'm so playful. I don't know. Things that carry over from childhood.

My father and mother used to tell me, "Whenever you see it, say good morning because it brings good luck." And that's why I do it.

Luck in advance because José was moved to spend some time with us; he risked coming back and everything went well. He leaves just after coffee. "The tortillas are from noon yesterday," I tell him as I serve him a little skillet with beans. "Don't worry. Don't go through the trouble of making them by hand early in the morning just to please me."

"I'm sorry that you don't have fresh tortillas to eat, especially now that you can't come home for lunch or even for supper." While I talk to him he has been looking at me in the candlelight. Because it's not dawn yet. At this time of the year the sun rises late—at five you still can't see your own fingers. One has to light a candle because it's hard to talk in the dark. Not to see another person's mouth moving, not to see their eyes, it's like talking with the dead. The dead can talk in the dark because they've gotten used to it little by little there six feet under. The dead are made for that, to live in the shadows. We living people are something else. "I wonder where I've left the matches," I say while I look for my apron. "Forget it, daylight is coming soon," he tells me.

"I'm still going to have to make a fire so you can leave all warm inside; I'm going to make coffee and you're not going to eat cold beans."

"Don't bother yourself; you have enough work, what with taking care of the kids all day." That's how he is; he doesn't get upset about anything. He used to be a little difficult, now he's changed. And while I watch him eating in the candlelight I keep quiet, not saying a word. It's time to say goodbye. "I won't be back for three days," he says. And then, "That's why I came home to sleep last night."

And I don't ask him anything. Because right at the moment when I was about to ask him something, our youngest child begins to cry. "You see what a crybaby he is?" "It must be worms," he tells me.

And I tell him, "You ought to get me some snake powder." And he gets angry: "There you go with your home remedies; you know that medicine is best." "Yes, I gave him a little something that I bought a while ago but it hasn't done any good," I tell him. "Well, keep giving it to him until it takes effect," he says.

"Medicine is so expensive—what used to cost ten cents is now two for twenty-five. I bought four packets of bismuth compound and I've only got one left," I explain.

"I'm going to give you twenty-five cents that I have left over, and go buy some more." And I ask him, "Aren't you going to be left with nothing?" "I don't need it because what am I going to spend it on if from work I go to the hills?" he replies.

"Go on, then," I say, and hold out my hand.

And I keep quiet again, without saying a word. I like to see him eat with gusto. He leaves the pot clean. Darkness is dangerous for everyone.

I like sunshine.

Life gets harder and harder. They say we have a lot of people in this country. And the most abundant are the poor. Hordes of poor people everywhere. But what can we do? What are we guilty of? That is why there's so much

51

hunger in the villages and everywhere. Well, I don't think life should be that way. "What's important is to be aware that one is poor," Chepe tells me repeatedly. "And what good is that?" I ask him. And he replies that only that way will we become strong enough to claim, to demand that which we have a right to. Everything else is a farce. What we must always insist on is the rights of the poor.

The people from here, the Kilometer, have always thought clearly, even though there are those who drag their feet everywhere.

The foremen on the plantations are the real snakes; they're always kissing up to the landowners.

From the plantations we get work but also misery. The plantation is nearby, less than two and a half miles away; we've lived off it all our lives, it's true.

It's also true that the plantation has prospered thanks to us. We've made it work. Before the road wasn't even paved. It was dusty in the summer and muddy in the winter; not even mules could pass along it during the rainy season, around September. We used to be isolated.

And lets look at the plantations now. All the plantations in these parts are linked by paved roads. They drive their cars on them with no difficulty.

We have never been envious. I don't remember that sin ever being in our hearts. What children say isn't true: that if envy were dye we'd all be colored; that's pure nonsense. The problem has nothing to do with envy but with necessity.

They forget that without our hands there's no sowing, no weeding, no harvesting, no clearing of the fields. Machetes don't move by themselves.

The hands that move most are the hands of farmworkers. Some of us barely have the know-how to make a pair of

oxen pull a cart to buy or sell something in town. The landowners sure pass by rapidly in their jeeps and limousines,
so fast that they don't even see people traveling beside the
highways. We have talked about all these things with José.
And we don't feel pain in our souls when we talk about our
neighbor. We used to. We couldn't even think bad thoughts
because we believed we would be condemning ourselves.
For everything there was damnation. For everything there
was hell. For everything there was fire as punishment. Our
tongue was always tied by our fear of sin.

The road to Hell is paved with evildoers, they'd tell us.
And the evildoers were those who had bad thoughts. We
always wanted to be good. We believed that to be good was
to bow one's head, not to protest, not to demand anything,
not to get angry. No one had clarified these things for us.
On the contrary, we were always being offered a celestial
paradise. The reward for being good. To respect one's neighbor was really to respect the landowner. And to respect the
landowner was to conform to his whimsy. If there were no
beans to eat after working on the plantation, it was because
the landowner couldn't manage, the landowner was suffering
losses. If there were no hammocks to sleep in, it was because
the harvest had not left the landowner enough time to provide them. And there we were without food, waiting for
the afternoon or the evening to go home to eat, a whole
day without eating; or we'd go to sleep under the *pepetos*
trees in the coffee fields.

We used to confuse goodness with resignation. I chatted
about all these things with José. Just last night we talked,
taking advantage of the opportunity since time was running
out now that our men cannot even sleep at home. What a
barbarity. We women are going to get sick from so much

53

anxiety. That's the worst part of it, the torture they put us through: anxiety and restlessness. Who had made the rich so evil? The whole night almost, talking to him. All snuggled up, both of us wrapped up in the same Guatemalan blanket.

—Be quiet now because the children will wake up.

—They sleep like a log; not even thunder wakes them up.

We spend the night talking softly. Ear to ear.

—It's already late.

—Not really.

—Even the crickets are quiet now.

So it is that we keep quiet, in the dark, thinking about ourselves and our children, all huddled up over there. About the little ones, because the big ones live in their own homes with their own companions. We don't think about these much—they've succeeded in making a life for themselves. Sometimes they visit. Every hundred years.

Well, the truth is, I had two grownup children: Justino, who used to live near San Martín, until the tragedy which befell him. Since then we've been through a lot. And María Pía, living over by Ilobasco, the poor thing. At least Justino doesn't suffer anymore. He left us by ourselves. We could count on his support. Every two weeks he would bring us his few cents. "Mama, here . . . , take this." "Ah, child, don't sacrifice, help me with only what you can." "Don't worry about me, Mama." And all those things that one appreciates in a son. He was younger than María Pía. A difference of five years, perhaps because God didn't want us to have children during that time, except for one who died of diarrhea when he was eight or nine months old. Now he would be twenty-six years old, only a year and a half older than Justino and four years younger than María. The poor thing, I couldn't even put a cross on his grave. It was so long ago that already it seems like a dream. I didn't even cry for him. He was so tiny you couldn't feel affection for him as a son yet. And besides, they suffer so much when their foreheads sink in, one would prefer they go and join the angels. Because that's what the priests from the missions who showed up around here once a year used to say. The neighbors were so good they gave us crepe paper to cover the heads of the children who accompanied Manuel de Jesús to his final resting place. That was his name, Manuel de Jesús. At least we were able to sing to him so that he wouldn't contaminate the angels with sadness.

After Justino it was as if God didn't want to bless us with more children until many years later. Now that I'm old I've had three more: one who is seven, another who is four and the baby who has been up and kicking for almost two years now.

Sometimes I grieve for the little ones, because one can deprive oneself of beans and eat salted tortillas, but children can't miss their little meals, at least curd or cottage cheese and beans. Even though there hasn't been enough lately. It is worth it to sacrifice for them. And yet they are the ones who make you suffer the most. If there isn't anything to eat, one gets desperate. "And today what am I going to give them?" And don't even ask about when they get sick.

It's better to be sick myself, because children suffer so much and the worst thing is that around here there isn't any medicine. Or sometimes there isn't enough money to buy even a balm. That's why it's better to prefer home remedies, such as chicken fat, iguana lard, snake powders, *guarumo* leaves or fox lard. In sum, all those things that give children some relief, even though they say it's better to get away from the custom of using things that are not from the drugstore. That's what the priests say. And we listen to them. Well, in any event, there aren't any doctors around here. I, at least, and I thank the Lord, don't know about doctors; I don't know what they're like.

Even though José has told me, "If the kids had a doctor to treat them, they wouldn't die just like that." We have never had that kind of assistance. And often I think: and if there were a doctor around here, with what money would we pay him, since we hear they're so expensive. I ask myself these questions. Or I ask José.

"The thing is to have free medicine," José tells me. "Oh, but that's impossible since everyone must charge in order to support himself," I tell him. "But free medicine is different, like in hospitals," he says. And as I don't allow myself to be convinced so easily, I respond, "Yes, but in hospitals they charge a minimum fee. That's why some people don't like to go to hospitals; they prefer to die at home and not in the city, because besides spending money for the bus you have to give money to the hospital, and where will it come from if you don't have any. And the cadavers, they take them to the morgue where they are butchered, or if not that, the doctors themselves keep the cadavers to learn more."

And that's how I go on contradicting José and he has the patience to go on explaining things to me. That's why I say, more than anything else Chepe has opened my eyes. And what's more, today I don't complain as much as before, because that awareness of being poor that José talks about begins to grow on you. No one is so hardened as to pretend not to understand. It's better to suffer in silence, and also to know what to do when they try to trick us. That's why we must learn so many things, so as not to live with our eyes shut. "We must save ourselves for ourselves."

Lately José has learned many things—you see, the poor man is interested in the problems of the community. I say it that way, because with all the work he has to do, he is still interested in others. "One has to help people so that they themselves will recognize their own problems," he tells me.

And I appreciate that quality in him. Others also appreciate it. They know he's looking out for the good of everyone. He's not an egotist. And if the truth must be told, he doesn't mince words. "I pray that nothing happens to Chepe, It's enough that I've lost Justino . . . and that María Pía suffers so much having been left without a husband since they made him disappear."

I think about all of this. And he says to me, "Don't worry, if those of us with understanding failed to act, we would all be in real trouble." "Yes, I won't worry," I tell him, so as not to add my problems to the lot.

Well, as I say, one is not made of stone. Justino's death destroyed me, why should I lie? It left me feeling like a piece of wood. At least with María Pía there's hope that Helio will return; he'll probably turn up. At least that's the hope that my granddaughter Adolfina gives me.

She comes here once in a while when she feels like it. She's a very intelligent child. She hasn't studied much, only up to the fifth grade, but I wonder where she's learned so many things. She's a brilliant little thing. She comes and

57

helps me draw water from the well. She and the children take the kernels off the ears of corn, and, playing at playing, they fill a basket. She's very close to us; she doesn't forget her grandparents. Now, since Justino's death, she comes more often. She speaks just like Chepe. "Don't worry, Grandmother, someday we're going to get our reward and the poor will not suffer anymore." Where does she get her ideas? I don't know. She's barely fifteen years old.

The only thing concerning her that I don't like is that, because she comes so often now and has grown nicely, a bad man might take a fancy to her. Around here there's no danger because we all know each other, but because she comes from so far away—from Ilobasco—the dangers are many for her at her age. And she's not ugly. That's what I'm afraid of.

When I tell her my worry, she only laughs. That's how young people are nowadays. You have to be understanding.

"Look, Grandmother, I've come to help you with the corn and to draw water, and also to have a vacation, please believe me. Well, you know, you never go out anymore, and my mother can't come; at least you have your granddaughter." That's the way she is.

"Don't take it personally. For me you're not a problem. I worry for you and your mother, that you won't get more bad news, what with all you've suffered. You should know that the little help you give me isn't as much as the joy I feel at seeing you here. I only say that because of all the bad things that have been happening; today no one is safe, not even in their own home." And seated on a bag of corn, her legs spread and her skirt falling over her feet, and with her innocent smiles, she works with the corn while I speak. A May flower about to bloom. That's the way Adolfina is.

She resembles José, something about the way she looks at you and her manner of saying things. Very sure of her words. Strong character. Qualities she was born with.

"Grandmother, I'm thinking of taking you to Ilobasco for a day, for a change of scenery, what do you say? You need to see your daughter and your other grandchildren; as soon as I earn a little money in the coffee harvest, I'll come get you." She's always joking. I have never gone farther than Chalate. God forbid!

7 A.M.

That's how Chalatenango has been since I can recall: tranquil, without big problems, only household ones, without robberies or delinquency. My mother says she always remembers it as having been a peaceful place. The last killing took place about forty years ago, when I was just a child. A man showed up here asking for work. "And what work could we give him!" says my mother. Finally he succeeded in getting a job near the Detour, at a manor house that used to be there. He hadn't been working a month when they brought the authorities down on him. They said he was an enemy of democracy. Who knows what they were talking about, because the man didn't bother anyone. The only thing he could be charged with was that he had a shotgun and would go out shooting white-winged pigeons or *tepescuintles*. My mother still remembers the blond stranger tall as a coconut palm, the barrel of his shotgun lodged on his shoulder.

And since he had no papers, the authorities told him he was as much as guilty, and since he didn't submit but resisted, well, right there they left him stretched out from an ass-whipping.

Rubenia Fuentes:

—I'll never forget it, child, you should have seen how they beat him. They gave it to the poor blond man for all they were worth.

Guadalupe Fuentes:

—And why were they so cruel, Mother?

Rubenia Fuentes:

—God only knows. What's certain is that you know you better not fool around with the authorities.

Guadalupe Fuentes:

—But you've told me that he didn't do anything to anyone, he only went out hunting.

Rubenia Fuentes:

—Well, that's the thing: you shouldn't give the authorities the slightest excuse because they have to act drastically. That's what they're paid for, they earn a salary.

Guadalupe Fuentes:

—They're not paid to kill honest people, to shoot for no good reason.

Rubenia Fuentes:

—Ah, my little girl, then why do you think they give them those big guns that look like tree branches and are larger than they themselves? To shoot, baby, to shoot. Because if they don't, that gives rise to talk that the authorities are useless, are nothing more than decoration.

They say he died instantly; what's for sure is that people in the neighborhood didn't get involved because back then there was so much talk of communism and the authorities were furious. "The Indians had rebelled, and they weren't going to forgive that even if it meant wiping out our entire population here." That's what my mother used to tell me. It was a little after 1932. "You can't imagine how terrible those days were. One couldn't even own a stamp with a saint on it because they believed that the prayers printed on the back were Communist slogans, and we had to burn the Virgin of Refuge, the Holy Child of Atocha, and even the Savior of the World." And I tell you things were bad. "You even had to be careful how you breathed so they wouldn't think you were grieving for a death and therefore presume that you had a dead Communist relative. More than forty thousand people died in those days." And I tell you that fortunately she saved herself and my father. She explains to me that in Chalate there were no uprisings because there were no coffee plantations, nor were there many workers and no one got rebellious here. They were lucky then, I tell you. "May the Lord protect me, you would have been left without a father, because all males were presumed to be Communist," she tells me. "Since there are no large coffee plantations around here, life is more peaceful— one eats when there's something to eat; for us poverty is a blessing," she continues. "I've never heard such things in my life," I tell her.

The guardsmen dragged him to the Detour; the mules they had ridden were there. The corpse was buried near here or the buzzards ate it. The authorities were laughing as they left.

One could see the laughter in their eyes, the only place where they are allowed to laugh.

Because the authorities cannot laugh. It is prohibited; at least they never laugh with their mouths. They're made to denounce, interrogate and capture. Laughing is a weakness. They themselves say, "Laughter abounds among fools." An official must not show any weakness before a civilian, otherwise he'll thereby lose precisely his authority. The authorities are short on words; they don't want to lose their strength by speaking to civilians. They act. That's the only way they can defend property, which is sacred. That's why many of them are paid by landowners. How big a bonus they get depends on how well they behave. Desolate farms, profitable fields.

My mother has told me all these things.

The plantations around here are large; one never knows how far they extend. If one stops atop a wall or a cliff, everything the eye can see belongs to one owner. Even the horizon is theirs. And the sky, too. The authorities guard the land, but who would steal anything from the plantation if only brush can be seen in all directions? Well, there's corn, but may a bolt of lightning strike anyone of us who tries to steal even a single ear.

The authorities are there instead of the owner of the plantation. I have never seen the owner of the plantation, but the authorities, I always see them. The owners of the plantations never come around. They only zoom by the Detour in their cars, in their jeeps. But don't let anyone dare to plant a little patch of land, heaven help him. No one had better cut down a tree; a *tamarindo* being a *tamarindo* isn't worth much, but you can't take it without permission. And there are times when one doesn't see a single soul around; one can get the itch to sneak in and steal a mango or an avocado, because sometimes one gets an urge for something, when one sees a fruit fallen to the ground, if only for the fun of it. But that is dangerous since one can

never know where the authorities will appear. And how they
shoot. One can't even see them; those big animals hit from
far away, they might be hiding in the underbrush or behind
a rock. Sometimes they climb the mango trees to eat mangoes and then they take a nap there in the branches.

Sometimes they give us firewood. Why should I lie?

—The owner says that entering the plantation to collect
firewood is allowed.

—Thank you, Señor Agent. I'll tell the others.

—But you have to hurry because it's only for today. Later
don't say that we are mean.

—No, Mr. Agent.

That way it's all right because we have permission. This
happens when it's almost winter, when they're about to set
fire to the land. During the cicada season and Holy Week.
There we walk among the *pepeto* trees, careful to step out
of the way of droppings. Well, even though they don't do
any harm, it's never good to let oneself be dirtied by in-
significant vermin.

—Goodbye, Lupita . . .

—Goodbye, sister . . .

—Come keep me company.

—Where are you going, sister?

—To cut firewood. Today they've given permission; come
get in on it.

—And how did you know, sister?

—The authorities came by and told Don Sebastián, who
sent us word.

—Wait for me, then, sister. I'm going to put on something,
but come on in, don't stay outside as if you weren't my
friend.

—Bring something even if it's only a rag so that you won't be pricked by thorns.

—Thanks, sister. I think Chepe left the rag around here.

—With your permission, then.

—Pull up a stool and sit down.

—And the children, sister, your godchild . . .

—They're running around in the yard, but we'd better not tell them because they'll get upset and will want to tag along.

—I'd better not sit down, Sister Lupita, because I won't feel like getting up again. I'd better wait here, but hurry up.

—Don't be impatient; I'm almost ready.

That's why that poor blond man must still be wandering around here in search of his soul; they didn't even give him a proper burial, and if buzzards ate him, at least his bones deserve to be buried. Maybe they were eaten by dogs, because my mother says that in the time around 1932 dogs used to eat corpses—there was so much hunger that not even animals could find enough to eat, not even avocados, which is the favorite food of dogs. There was total misery. And the worst is that certain people who made a living raising pigs couldn't sell them because the pigs also ate cadavers and the people refused to eat pork. This all happened in Santa Tecla, my mother says.

Well, as I was saying, the death of the blond man was the last. In almost forty years.

Maybe that's why we were resigned to Justino's death—it was the will of God and of those bandits.

I don't even like to recall it. His death is still fresh.

MARIA PIA

*I'm also from around these parts, I'm the wife of Helio
Hernández. He was captured by the National Guard. They
picked him up and tortured him, they hit him with rifle
butts on the back and on the head.*

*He was coming from sleeping in the hills and ran into
them.*

*He was with Emilio Ramírez, who was knocked down
fast. Helio managed to run but he got tangled up in some
vines and tripped.*

*There five guardsmen fell on him, beating him all over
with the rifle butts. In such a way as to leave him motionless.
"Murderers, leave him alone," I screamed.*

—Why did you run, you coward?

*We were going out, we were in the street when they were
coming with the boys. I was carrying a fifteen-month-old
baby in my arms. As they approached us they all began to
cut switches of guayabo and as soon as they reached us
they grabbed us and beat us with their switches.*

Helio and Emilio, all banged up, watching. With their hands tied behind their backs. Then the guardsmen started kicking us.

—Whores! We're going to finish off all of you!

And we shouted: "Leave us alone! We're not doing anything!"

Then they carried them to the bus stop, where there were other guardsmen waiting.

After a while they returned.

And as we continued down the street they followed us and kicked us; they grabbed my baby and whacked him so hard on the head as to knock him out of my arms. And then they whipped me on the back, on the head, all over my body, leaving me black and blue. Finally they let me go, when they had gotten tired, and returned to Helio and Emilio, still bleeding, even though someone had put a rag on their heads or maybe it was the guardsmen, who didn't want them to watch, but they really don't care who sees or doesn't see what they do. And when they got back they started hitting them again with rifle butts on the ears, in the back, while at the same time kicking them with pointed boots; the mouths of the guardsmen were drooling saliva— they were having such a good time. Helio finally fell from being hit in the head by a rifle butt.

He fell as if dead.

And the guardsmen told Emilio:

—Pick him up if he's your friend. Don't be a faggot!

Then Emilio squatted down to look at Helio because he couldn't even touch him, as his hands were tied behind his back.

Then Helio raised his hand as if wanting to get up; he seemed to be coming around.

And when he'd gotten up, wobbling, they started beating him with their rifle butts again.

Our screams were heard all over town until a crowd formed, wanting to know what was happening. Next they took them to the bus stop, this time dragging them as we followed. They left them on the ground and came after us.

And they told us: "And you, whores, what is it you want?"

—*Helio is my husband.*

—*What does that have to do with us, bitch. Just tell us your name!*

And he took out a little notebook. The one who gave the orders, the private. Then I noticed that he was Ticha's son, who had remained crouched at the bus stop as if ashamed that we might see him. I did some quick thinking: fortunately I had sent Adolfina to my mother's house. It's good that she wasn't a witness to all this. Luckily she had left.

—*You are María Pía . . .*

—*Yes, you know me, don't you?*

And the other one said:

—*Look what a rude whore!*

He looked as if he was going to hit me again with the switch.

And Ticha's son said:

—*Hey, you, leave her alone, don't hit her again; she's already had a good enough whipping.*

And the guardsman tells him: "Oh, no, my private! Because if you're a softy with these people, no one will be able to put up with them."

—*Yes, but enough! It would be better if we took these bastards away before there's a fuss.*

*Because the people of the town had gathered and were
asking what Helio and Emilio had done.
And I told them:*
—*They were on their way back from sleeping in the hills.
They sleep in the hills because someone reported them
as having gone to the demonstration at the Bank demanding lower prices for seeds and fertilizer. Well, they
came looking for them twice; that's why they decided to
go sleep in the hills. You see, the Guard always looks for
them at night, hoping to grab them at home instead of
having to capture them on the plantation, thereby compromising the owner. When it was all said and done, it
was the landowner who reported their going to San
Salvador, because several workers asked for that day off,
saying they were sick. And the foreman made a list and
gave it to the Guard. It wasn't by chance that they surrounded the houses of those who had gone to the Bank.*

*Just yesterday I went to Ilobasco to see them. I asked
to speak with Private Martínez, Ticha's son, but they
told me he was on assignment, and besides, who was I?
A guardsman took out a notebook to record my name
and I told him I was looking for Helio Hernández—it had
already been two weeks since they'd captured him.*

*And he asked me everything, even what I thought I
was going to die of. Noting it all down.*

*I went to the park to sit on a bench, there in front of
the jail, when I saw that William was coming out, a boy
who likes to accompany the Guard—I wonder why?—like
a mascot. I knew him because he used to come to the
village on errands for the guardsmen. Maybe he's an
apprentice? God only knows. And I shouted to him:*
—*William, William!*

Maybe he was going to run an errand—he lives in the Ilobasco jail. Since everyone knows him, I spoke to him without misgivings.

I ask him. When he has gotten closer, I ask him:
—William, have you seen Helio?
He starts to laugh. And he tells me:
—Sure, they've got him in there.
I ask him:
—Have you seen him yourself, William?
He answers:
—Well, where else could he be?
By now I've gotten up from the bench, upset. I ask him again:
—Have you really seen him, William?
He answers me:
—I swear I have . . .
I am so elated by William's good news that I ask:
—And, William, nothing has happened to him, right?
Still laughing, he tells me:
—Yes, the first days. They stuck them in a tub of water and chili peppers. Imagine how their wounds must have burned, they screamed; then they shoved a toothbrush with pepper back there, in their buttocks, and then into their mouths for them to brush their teeth with . . .
And I tell him:
—William, what I would like to do is see them . . .
But he doesn't stop talking:
—You should have seen how thirsty they were because they hadn't gotten water for several days, so the chief asked if they wanted some "Quaker Oats" refreshment and they said yes . . .

And since I no longer want to hear it, I ask him:

—But are they alive, William?

—Of course they are! Why should they be dead?

—Because one can't even see them! It's as if they'd disappeared!

But he continues:

—Helio grabbed the bottle because they couldn't stand the thirst and he put it to his mouth and guess how surprised he was to feel a fire in his mouth. You see, the bottle was filled with malathion, a poison given to animals. All of us laughed at Helio because he'd had a good swig of refreshment . . .

I try to have him stop, because I know he's making fun of me.

—William, for the love of life, tell me how Helio is . . .

Continuing to laugh, he tells me:

—Well, the last time he had the bone in his shoulder dislocated; what do they call it, the clavicle? As for Emilio? I think he kicked the bucket, he couldn't take the acid.

And I can't stand much more of this:

—Ay, they're so cruel and why don't they return the bodies. Emilio's mother is dying of anguish, and as for Helio, they should send him to the hospital or let us see him, me at least . . .

But he no longer heard me, because he ran off and I went back to the bus stop to go on home . . .

And now the result: upon returning, around six-thirty, I went to bed because I had a high fever and a headache. Well, at around ten o'clock they began knocking at our door and I asked them: "Who is it?" "Open up!" they shouted from outside. And again I said: "Who is it?" And they

71

answered: "Open the door! Or we're going to bust the shit out of it for you, it's the National Guard."

I knew the voice of Private Martínez, Ticha's son, and gathering all my strength I shouted at him: "Look, Mr. Private, I can't get up because I'm sick."

And they: "Open up or we'll bust the shit out of it!"

And the voice of a child: "Open up, Pía, open up little chickadee, pío, pío, pío."

It was William, the boy of the gardener.

Then I came and since I was trembling with fever I told my ten-year-old boy, "Look, son, get up." And he told me that he couldn't go out and open the door because he was afraid.

So then I yelled at them, "Wait, I'm going to get dressed."

And they told me: "Ah, so we're supposed to wait for you to get dressed, you shit?"

I grabbed my dress and as it was dark I put it on backwards. "Please wait," I told them while I lit a candle.

"We're not waiting for you; either open up or we'll bust the shit out of your door. We're already running out of patience," they told me.

I was straightening my dress when the door flew open, almost falling on me. I only had time to throw myself on the bed where my three children and I sleep together: a girl of seven, a boy of ten and a baby boy of fifteen months, or rather sixteen. Then they flipped the bed over on us and I fell with all the children on the corn, which was in the bin.

And they said: "Look, you dumb shit, why wouldn't you open the door?"

And I tell them, still sprawled over the corn and the

children screaming out of terror: "I'm sick. Leave me alone."

"Here's something to make you sick!" And I received the first blow of the rifle butt in the eye. I felt as if my eye had fallen out, and then they started in on my ribs and my back. And my girl cried out: "Stop hitting my mother!" She tried to scratch them, desperate, screaming, "Let go of her!" Then a guardsman raised his arm to hit her in the face, but I quickly put my arm up and the blow hit me so hard that it almost peeled the skin off my hand. Then another guardsman caught me off guard with a kick in the ribs.

Then Ticha's son said to me: "So you oppose authority? Just wait, because the worst is yet to come, you haven't seen anything." And my fifteen-month-old baby was crying but I wouldn't let go of him, so that they wouldn't kill me, because they would not shoot me with a child in my arms. As for my ten-year-old, I couldn't feel him, thrown as he was on top of the corn.

"Here you go," Ticha's son told me, and the kick caught me in the back. They whipped me about twenty times more. And at the end a kick in the foot that has left me lame. After that the private got up on the bed and began jumping on it, trying to break it, and the bed creaked, finally splitting apart. And then he comes and with a knife he began to slash the webbing of the bed, until he'd ruined it. He looked like a madman.

I had a small pot of corn standing on the floor. Private Martínez broke the pot, spilling all the corn.

Then they grabbed a new bag I had bought for the baby's clothes, and a bible, and carried them away. After that they went to my father-in-law's house and began to beat

73

on his door. And William shouted at him, "Aha! You old son of a bitch, now we're really going to cut off your balls." And my mother-in-law said, "But why, William?" And this one said: "Ah, old man, because that's why we've come, to cut off your head, quick and clean." So my father opened the door and they slammed their rifle butts in his chest. William only laughed.

Since then I haven't slept at home, you see, they told me that if they didn't kill me this time, they'd hang me the next. Now they've told me I have three choices: one, sell the house, the other, leave without selling anything, and the other, stay here, but they're going to kill all the women who remain alone in their houses. Well, since all the menfolk sleep in the hills, we are deserted at night. And I, without Helio now, am afraid during the day as well as the night. Now I too am going to sleep in the hills. At sundown I'm taking my children, a sleeping mat for them and some blankets for the cold. I feel safer now that all the men are going to sleep there.

The hills aren't bad, even though the mosquitoes and the cold sometimes don't let you sleep. When Helio shows up, I'm not going to feel so bad.

And I begin to think about life: William is only twelve and already a criminal. I knew him when he was just a child—he used to help carry things at the big store in Ilobasco. He was so attentive to the customers. Until he went to work for the Guard as a watchman.

It was a terrible week. The one I was most afraid for was my oldest daughter, but thanks to the neighbors they convinced her to spend a few days in Chalate, at the Kilometer, where my mother lives. I don't know what could have happened to her. I don't even want to think about it.

ADOLFINA

This road is in bad shape, the one joining the main road from the north. The pickup truck lumbering up the hill. A clunker spewing heavy exhaust fumes everywhere as if it were burning up. Whirlwinds of dust: "There goes your mother-in-law, there goes your mother-in-law." Just to ward off the devil, an old custom: my great-grandmother Rubenia says that the devil is present in whirlwinds. And I believe that my mother also believes a little in those things. Dust from the road settles on the branches of the trees, on the leaves, which during the summer become gray even though in the spring they are as green as can be and glimmer from being washed by rainwater. Pof-pof—that's how it sounds, like a beaten dog. The rocks on the road cause us to jounce in our seats. Traveling on Saturday is always a problem because one has to move in a crush of people and dust gets through the windows. The Doriana can't move because it's missing a wheel. All we need is for it to be stranded on the road! I just want to die. We're packed in like sardines. "Everyone off for a moment," shouts the gray-haired conductor to the gray-haired driver, so the gray-haired people must get off. It's the dust from the road. Fortunately, it only lasts for about a mile, then there's pavement, where the Doriana is waiting, and even though she's broken down, she moves like a bitch in heat down the road.

—A few friends have come by and have advised that you leave your house for a few days. I think the best place is your grandmother's.

—Ay, Mama, I don't think that's necessary.

—I'm telling you, you have to go. There's a reason why they said so.

—If we haven't done anything bad, Mama . . .

—After what happened at the Bank maybe the authorities are going to come to bother us. I'm sure. Your father says he agrees that you should go spend a week with your grandmother Lupe.

—Well, all right.

And directly before is the main highway, because around here it winds in and out like a snake. The huge cliffs that are seen while one climbs toward Chalate. Trucks full of cotton pickers descend to the coast. So much arid land around here, gray dust rising in whirlwinds. "There goes your mother-in-law, there goes your mother-in-law." We're all made of that dust. To think we're made of that dust and to it we shall return. That's what the priest says. Flesh turns into dust, only the spirit rises. The sky around here isn't even blue, just a cloud of dark dust.

—Too bad there isn't anyone to go with you.

—That's not necessary, I'll go alone.

—*Won't it be dangerous, my child?*

—*I've been in worse situations, Mother, that's for sure. I know how to take care of myself and I won't take any chances.*

—*What's really dangerous is for you to stay here.*

"*Chalatenango, my blessed land, warm little site of the Cuscatlán garden,*" *they taught me this song at school. I kind of like it, even though my father says it is the crappiest song that can be dedicated to a place like Chalatenango. My father is a little out of line and never has liked school songs. Or maybe he's right.*

I can't even eat a banana because dust sticks to it. And to think these people are sucking on oranges. Maybe they're thirsty and have no other choice. I'm carrying some bananas for my grandmother in my bag. Always when I come to see her I bring a certain kind of banana that's rare around these parts, where there are only the little ones. Or I bring her a couple of plantains. Plantains don't grow here, either.

Miraculously that bird appears. It is a kiskadee. "Cuiocuio," says the loud kiskadee, announcing its visit. My grandmother says the kiskadee also announces death. And my father says the opposite: that when the kiskadee makes cuio-cuio, what it's doing is announcing the death of our Lord; it's not really saying "cuio-cuio," but "Cristo fué." "*Haven't you noticed that you only hear the kiskadee at Easter or around Holy Week?*" *he asked me. And it's true. The kiskadee sings in the middle of the dry season. I think it's asking for water when it sings. And no one gives it any. Like the San Juan bells that ask for bread that no one gives. The kiskadee is perched on a little branch so high up the guanacaste tree that if it weren't for its song, you wouldn't know where to look for it. What I'm sure about is that the kiskadee announces visitors. I know that because when my mother is in the kitchen and she hears the kiskadee, she says: "Listen, company is coming." And the visitor arrives. Very well proven.*

—*Two weeks with my grandparents is a long time.*

—*Listen to me. After what happened to your Uncle Justino, you get out of here and don't come back for two weeks. Here's bus fare. Can't you see that your father can't even sleep at home; it's necessary to take precautions, daughter.*

—*Yes, I'm not denying that, I was only saying it's a long time.*

—*All right, but don't behave foolishly. I've said the last word on this. What's more, don't forget that some people know you participated in the Bank demonstration and in the occupation of the Cathedral.*

It is the only brave bird—it even fights hawks. It gets on top of them and rides their backs, and no matter how the hawk flips and turns, the kiskadee sticks to it. Fights between kiskadees and hawks are beautiful, because the hawk tries to flee and the kiskadee pursues it; they circle in the sky until the kiskadee catches up with the hawk and perches itself on the other's back. The hawk then says "cuerk-cuerk" and the kiskadee sings "Cristo fué," without dismounting its horse.

I wonder how many Christian souls are flying around in that whirlwind. In that cloud of dust raised by the Doriana. Sweat, streams of dirty water running down my body. Sweat mixes itself with dust. When I arrive, I'm going to take a bath. Dust in my clothes, in the handkerchief tied around my head. "Get off now or we'll all be crapped out with the Doriana," says the conductor. "Everybody off." That's why it's better to travel to San Salvador and from there

take the number 38, which goes to Chalate; it's more ex-
pensive but it's better. And since we're moving slowly the
driver shouts: "Everybody off." "Take it easy," someone
says. And the woman sitting next to me is carrying a child
in her arms. "I'm thirsty." "Ah, she talks." And she tells
her: "Be quiet, dear, we're almost there." "Ah, it's a girl."
"When we get to the Detour, I'll buy you a tamarindo
drink," she says to the girl. "Maybe she's dying of thirst,"
I say to her. "She's only pretending. Were we at home, she
wouldn't be asking for water so often. Before leaving, I
gave her a lot of water so that she wouldn't be a pest along
the way." That's how children are, I tell you. "The more
you spoil them, the more they misbehave; they can be such
a bore," she says. "If you want, give her this banana; who
knows how long we'll be stuck here." She grabs the banana
and peels it. "Here," she says to the little girl. She gives
her the whole banana. The girl eats it, every bit of it. Sitting
on a rock in the scorching sun. "Look, don't start pissing."
"No," I tell her, "I've put a rag underneath her; if you
want, I'll help you with her." "Thanks," and she hands her
over to me. "They're such a nuisance," she says. Again I
see the kiskadee; it must be the same one, it has followed
me. It will get to the Kilometer first. It's going to sing to
my grandmother and then my grandmother will say:
"Listen to the kiskadee: it's the sign that someone is com-
ing." That's why the kiskadee is like a messenger. He
brings and carries messages. The sun makes me sleepy. The
little girl goes to sleep on me. "If you want, give her to me
and I'll help you." I wake up when the conductor yells
again: "Everybody on!"

    In truth, I was never really asleep. "Thanks for the help,"
the woman tells me.

9:30 A.M.

From the beginning I noticed that Pijiriche seemed nervous. "I don't know what's come over this animal." "Get out," I tell it. Because I was tired of its whining. He runs underneath the stool, and in a little while he jumps up again and darts desperately all over the place. "The fleas are driving him crazy." I know it's not fleas, because only a few days ago I washed him with DDT. I even grabbed a stick and told him that if he kept on whining I'd whip him.

A short time later the authorities appeared. Pijiriche had gotten their scent. These sad people don't even ask permission. I hear the door crash open all of a sudden and they're coming in. "What is it you want?"

"Does Adolfina Guardado live here?" they ask me. "We want to know if this is the house of Adolfina Guardado." they say. "We're looking for her."

No Adolfina Guardado lives here. "Get out, Pijiriche."

Guadalupe Fuentes lives here. "What can I do for you?"
And they answer me by taking out a little notebook and
reading, "It's right here—this is her house." The voice of
an announcer, the one who reads the news at twelve. A
raspy voice comes from a cave full of bats. From a deep
and dark hole. If it had not been for Pijiriche's company,
my feet would have been trembling. Adolfina's last name
is Hernández.

"It would be better if you didn't try to fool me." "I'm not
tricking you my granddaughter's last name is Fuentes,
Adolfina Fuentes." High leather boots, halfway up their
calves, and bandolier belts. The worst are those monsters
they carry on their shoulders. These are the famous automatics they talk about. Iron helmets as in films about the
Germans. And a thing like a radio on their backs. These
people are very serious. They're studying to be President.
And how can they fail, with monsters that "shoot a ton of
lead a minute," as José says. If they hit you in the leg, they
rip the leg right off; if they hit you in the arm, the arm is
blown away, they tear the arm right off. So how can they
fail. As for being intelligent, you know they're not that because educated people don't go around getting involved
with the authorities. We know that much from our own experience. More than one person here has gone looking for
work as an official, and they aren't the best people. That's
the truth or my name isn't Guadalupe Fuentes de Guardado,
wife of Chepe, José.

"Look, we aren't interested in her real last name. The
person we're looking for is a relative of yours named
Adolfina; you people all change your names."

"They say that the rifles they carry are the best in the

world; not even in movies, Guadalupe, not even in movies can you see them because they're so modern and the movies we get here are older than the hair on your ass," José says.

My granddaughter Adolfina is the daughter of María Pía Guardado Fuentes, my daughter, married to Helio Hernández. I know that to lie is a sin and a sin is costly with these people, so if they tell me a name and it's not the right one, well, I have to tell them the truth. Nowadays not only does God punish but so do these men. It would be better to pretend not to understand; maybe they're mistaken about who they're after. Or better yet, it's a dream, how could these people be asking about my granddaughter? It must be a mistake. She's only a child. It would be better had they asked for me or for José. Because, after all, adults can be bad but children can't. Since when were they inspired by the idea to mess with innocent children? Even if I were a scorpion, I couldn't let my children be eaten. Grandchildren are also our children.

They tell me that there is no mistake, that it's precisely Adolfina who is involved here. I give up.

—She's over at the Detour buying salt and a little cheese for the baby.

—Which Detour?

—At the store of Don Sebas.

How to talk to them? Maybe they'd like hot tortillas stuffed with a little something. Too bad the fire has gone out and that today I didn't use the *comal*.

I can see them sweating from the hot sun; the sun is oppressive. And they've come on foot from who knows where. They always leave their jeep far away—it's a custom they have. They love to walk because that way the people can see them better, showing off their tall bodies, their uniforms the color of cow dung, their leggings and their big automatic monsters. They're all tall and strong. Not by chance; they're well fed. They always travel in pairs. There are two of them, but other pairs are probably lurking around. Talking to each other with those gadgets that look like radios. They're probably talking from the jeep.

—We'll wait for her, then.

And they stand waiting in the little hallway, pull out handkerchiefs smelling of sweat and dirt. One of them wipes his brow. Another inspects the hallway and then the banana trees outside, searching through the bunches of bananas.

—Sit down if you want.

They say no. Something sticks in my throat, a hook that has reached my heart and is being pulled upward. Not for me—when you've reached our age you've lived a lot. For Adolfina more than anything.

They always claim self-defense. They kill and that's the end of it, then and there. Self-defense. This is serious business.

"Perhaps you would like a little drink of water?" They pretend not to hear me. It's cool; you can even see the red jar sweating. Water, full of life. Fresh, cool water from the well.

They don't say a word. In cases such as this it's best to commend oneself to God. I've almost swallowed the pinch of tobacco; I spit the black saliva.

These people always bring bad luck. That's why I've offered them water—to drive a little of the bad luck away. Besides, one shouldn't refuse water to anyone.

Around the fireplace. This old fan no longer cools. I'm going to pour a little more gas on the firewood. Hot air from outside gets in and blows out the fire. If they refuse favors, it's because they don't want to seem ungrateful later. They don't want to owe anything to anyone.

The dry sticks always pop and snap like a bunch of firecrackers. Fire consumes them little by little. The tall flames flicker. The hot red fire; the thicker wood begins to burn. Now I can sit down on the bench. The shiny seat of *madrecacao* wood.

—That woman hasn't come yet.

I hear them speaking in low voices. I explain:

—She has three children with her and the youngest is still a babe in arms. She must be having trouble getting here.

I don't care if they know that I'm listening to them. My duty is to explain things to them. They don't even pay any attention to me. A lump descends from my throat to my ankles. That's why we say our knees are knocking when we're afraid, I say or I think. A trembling of legs. Everything is imaginary, because if you can talk about fear you won't feel it, if you don't owe it anything you won't fear it. A slight fear for the child. Because she's so young. Adolfina likes rice and one tries to buy it whenever she comes. Considering the effort she must make to get from her home to the Kilometer, it's worth it to make the sacrifice and buy rice. White smoke rises from the skillet. Smoke from the Vatican. The ashes float toward the beams supporting the roof of the hut. The beams of the hut that have been blackened by soot. They're more than fifteen years old; it's a miracle they haven't come tumbling down. Such things will give you gray hair before your time. The rice is drying out; it needs more water. And my hands are like spiders with five legs. Worrying will make you skinny.

Worrying and bad thoughts.

They're going to think I'm crazy. Instinctively one makes the sign of the cross. "I hope these people don't think I'm doing this because I'm afraid of them." At my age one isn't afraid. Well, it's true I'm not that old. What happens is that you begin having children when you're still a child. I went to live with José when I was fifteen. No one would know that I'm going on forty-five. Life is rough.

Would you like a little drink of water? I think again. It's better not to offer these people anything; they're ingrates. From where does all this salt come through the eyes? With this dirty apron you shouldn't wipe even your hands. José gave it to me two years ago. It's too much; they're bound to notice that my eyes are getting red.

By now they must be getting angry.

But no. They are angry. They're not becoming anything. That's what distinguishes them. I can see it in their eyes. Their wrinkled brows. Who could have invented the authorities? They're furious, no doubt about it. In spite of being well fed, their skin is real dry. Sometimes I think they're sad. Because—why deny it?—we know moments of happiness in our poverty; sure, it's only a matter of knowing how to put a good face on things.

"No, no, we don't want any," they tell me when I offer them my water. They wouldn't lose anything by saying yes. Water is sacred and one shouldn't deny it even to the devil.

—We have canteens with drinking water.

—I was offering it to you just in case . . .

If they think I have some ulterior motive they'll shit

on it. That's their problem. It's one thing to be afraid of them and another to pay them attention.

"Come this way, dog."

Because Pijiriche might try to approach them. Don't tell me Pijiriche isn't intelligent! Under other circumstances he would have barked. It's as if he'd figured things out.

—Pijiriche, lie down.

—And where could this bastard dog have come from?

—You see, now they've insulted you for being so dumb.

If you bark at them, you're a dead dog. "Pijiriche," I shout this time. Because he's walking over to the man.

—This son of a bitch, he pissed on my boot!

—Bad dog!

I should have known. He goes flying through the air from one kick. "Come here. Now he's broken your ribs; you deserve it." That's what he gets for being stupid. And to think I said he was such an intelligent dog.

And laughter starts to well up inside me. Because of the way the guardsman stomps his boot. "All right. Go lick your wounds under the banana tree. That way you won't cause me any more trouble."

The laughter anew. The laughter returns. "What's the matter with that old whore?" I had it coming on account of that fucking dog. But the real son of a bitch is the guardsman. And the truth is that I'm not laughing because Pijiriche pissed on the man. It's true. What happened was that I remembered one of José's jokes. A visitor arrives at the house of General Gómez, the famous general, who's reclining in a hammock. The visitor sits on a chair under which the general's dog is lying. All of a sudden the visitor inadvertently lets go a little fart. And to hide his shame the

visitor blames the dog, uttering as a reproach, "Dog!"
And he looks under the chair. And the general only rocks
in his hammock, smoking his cigar. Again the visitor lets
go another little fart, and he leans toward the dog and
says, "Dog!" The general continues rocking peacefully in
his hammock. When the visitor lets loose yet a third little
fart, the general is ready for him and says, "Dog, get out
of there, that man is going to shit on you."

It's Chepe Guardado's favorite joke.

—That old woman is crazy.

Just look at the grief that a pissy dog can cause. And my
mother used to say, "Your mouth is always open, you're always going around laughing." And it's true. When I was a
child I'd laugh at anything. "Your teeth are going to freeze,"
my mother would say; or, "A girl who laughs a lot is begging
for a man." But these things went right over my head. I was
only ten years old. And only four years later I was with
Chepe and I hadn't even flirted with him because he was
older than I was. Things were arranged by my mother. José
took me away from home when I was barely fifteen, so I
never had time to enjoy life in a certain way because when
one is committed to a man, one has to forget everything
else. And what's more, from early on I was pregnant with
María Pía and had to raise children and get serious because one's commitments grow. Grownups can go without
eating. Children are another matter. And then a little while
later, while I was still nursing, I'd go to the coffee field. To
Santa Tecla with José. And soon thereafter the second one
came. And that's how life is.

More than a few times I kidded around with José, well,
I won't say I wasn't coquettish; I used to put little flowers

in my hair, and when he'd arrive, he'd take them out and begin nervously to pick them apart, and even though he was a lot older than I was, I always liked him, from the beginning. Certainly, I never imagined that it would all end up with him being my husband.

We got married. My eyes would cross when he came to visit me or I would trace little drawings in the air or fidget and fidget in front of him, until my mother would say to me, "Girl, why are you so antsy?" And Chepe would look at me.

And I would look at him.

Later one gets tired, it's true. Goodbye laughter, children arrive. It's time for the coffee harvest and one must round up the children and take off with hardly a mat or blankets. Not even clothes because one always wears the same clothes, for laughing and crying. And that's where that song comes from, "So You're Wearing the Same Clothes." Well, what are you going to do if you live in poverty? Only complain and complain? As long as things are unclear, that's how it is.

Well, all right, the way the authorities can fuck one over; we know where that's coming from.

And we know why they harass us, why they get angry. Well, once I asked Chepe what being aware meant, and it's that, more or less. To know why. And maybe that's why I laugh so much, because they'd like you to be all fucked over, without knowing what to do about it. It's true, I'm worried about the child, and I would give my life for her.

But I refuse to be provoked into doing something dumb.

José has advised me many times: one must be respectful, as much as one can, to the authorities. None of this considering them our enemies. Don't provoke them, don't run from them because they'll shoot. Especially if you notice them giving you aggravation for the hell of it, they want something. They're watching for your reaction so as to take advantage of you and fuck you over. Don't fall into their traps. You can achieve all this without messing yourself over, that's what José tells me.

THE AUTHORITIES

We'd never eaten with knife and fork; the luxury is un-imaginable—they shine as if they were made of silver or gold. Well, we had only eaten with wooden spoons, the kind we make ourselves, that are also used for sipping fermented black corn and that you need to scrape every so often with a piece of glass. The bad thing about silver spoons is that they burn your mouth, while a wooden spoon doesn't have that defect; one can drink atol *hot and nothing will happen.*

Even less had we eaten on tablecloths, like the cloth that tortillas are wrapped in, only bigger, with colored tassels around the edges; and the material isn't cotton but more like silk, so fine it's hard to imagine, it feels like velvet, the feathers of a dove. And not to mention the chairs. Well, it's all a paradise. What more can we ask for?

And even if it's true that the trainer treats us badly. One of those gringos *who knows a lot. All told, I wouldn't change my life for anything, God be my witness. We eat meat every day; as I wasn't used to it at first, it was bad for me, I'd get stomachaches. Another thing: we don't even have to eat tortillas; it's a thing that at the beginning caused me problems. They only give you bread with something they call margarine or garlic butter—ah! what's the use of telling you, I know you won't understand. The other trainer, a little Chinese man who doesn't speak Spanish, only gibberish, tells us, "You live like kings," so that we'll realize how well off we are. Well, you can't even understand what he says, "To live king, tell, tell." We want to laugh at the way his tongue gets tangled up, but we keep real quiet because heaven shield us from this little Chinese man. As a trainer, he sure is good.*

Imagine, take mashed potatoes, for example, which I didn't know shit about. I'll explain it to you: it's something like mashed corn but it's potatoes, all beaten up or ground up, you wouldn't believe it. At first it's disgusting; you can barely swallow it because it's insipid and they put sprigs of coriander on top of it. But, you see, it becomes a dish for the gods. The Chinese man says, "God's dish." I would have liked to have brought you a little to try, but since they register everything we have as we leave, it wouldn't have been good for them to find mashed potatoes in my suitcase. I don't even know why they call it purée. Look, I'll tell you something to be frank, and pardon my language, purée looks like shit except it smells like semen. Can you imagine being forced to eat it? And after a while it's something you get used to. They say this food was invented in France. I don't know. The people in those countries are so inventive.

Mornings, we have orange juice and a kind of milk called yogurt. Well, the little juice is all right, but the yogurt,

*what the fuck is that? pardon my expression; well, so you'll
know, if the purée smells like semen, yogurt is almost semen
itself. And you have to swallow it like worm medicine. At
first, real carefully, I'd hold my nose to get it down; now it's
enough for me to concentrate on how good it is for you and
it goes down without any problem. It's like tossing down a
shot of cane liquor, see, two or three mouthfuls without
tasting it. Otherwise you can't keep it down, and then:
sure punishment. Once someone couldn't keep it down no
matter how hard he tried. And the director told us, "Look,
motherfuckers, I don't want to see or hear bullshit like
that, keep that in mind." What can you do? As far as everything else is concerned, we live like kings.*

We have to be well fed, the gringo *tells us, so we can
defend the country. In exchange for these pleasures, we
cannot let these people down. One must be ready to defend
the country against its enemies even at the expense of our
own brothers. And, though it's unnecessary to say so, even
at the expense of our mother. This might seem like an
exaggeration, but the Western world is in danger and we
know that the worst danger to the Western world is what
they call "the people." The trainer shouts, "Who is our
worst enemy?" And we shout, "The people!" And so on and
so on, "Who is the worst enemy of democracy?" And we
all respond, "The people!" Louder, he says. And we shout
with all our might, "The people, the people, the people."
I'm telling you this in the strictest confidence, of course.
They call us the Special Forces.*

*They pump this into us. It's true; well, if it weren't true,
they wouldn't spend so much to allow us this much luxury.
Think about it, even the cheese is different; the cheese we
eat is red on the outside and yellow inside, like a jewel.*

Well, when in my motherfucking life would I have dreamed of things like these? No, not everyone gets as much. Only the Special Forces. All our instructors are foreigners, except the director, but he's hardly ever around—he comes only once in a while, to inquire about our discipline, how our training is going. And we all must shout in unison, "Fine, for our fatherland, Chief!" This I'm telling you in confidence; take real care not to tell anyone.

And we have instructors in things you'd never imagine, for example, in the arts; yes, that's what they're called, the martial arts. The Chinese man teaches the martial arts, even how you can gouge someone's eye out with your thumb. And another class called psychology, which is to say, how you can make people suffer by the mere use of words, because you know it isn't always necessary to use force—often there are people who understand only words. This science of psychology has something to do with electric apparatuses.

Only by being tough can we save endangered democracy. But you better be careful that none of this slips out, brother, because you know that what's foolishly discussed isn't worth a damn thing. And then I'd say you invited me to have a few drinks just to get me to talk. No, no, don't be afraid, let's have one for the road. Brother, I'm inviting you, don't get up and leave me now. Don't start falling asleep on me now, because you know if you're not careful, you'll get fucked over.

Get this, the gringo says that the soul of the people has been poisoned. They're brainwashed. This is something scientific, but in these parts, because we're backward countries, we don't understand. It's not that we're stupid but that we're a country of illiterates, lugs, as they say; well, because we were born lazy. We had the bad luck of being conquered by the Spanish, who were nothing but drunkards, while up there in the north arrived the English, who are all great workers. What's more, the English killed off the Indians but the Spaniards didn't. That was the big mistake. Because, you know, and I don't mean to speak ill about our race, but we Indians are all fucked up; we want everything to fall from heaven into our laps. We're all very conformist. Look at me. Well, if I hadn't had the courage to go to the city, I'd be like you, no offense intended, brother. I'd be living from hand to mouth like you, eating shit; by the way, that stuff you've been eating can't be called food. Get this, in the United States, for example, corn is only for pigs and horses, and to think that here we settle for tortillas and salt.

As I was saying, it's pure bad luck; even in this business of religion we've come out badly. While up there, in the United States, the real Christ arrived with those modern churches they call Jehovah's Witnesses and Mormons, with handsome blond ministers who are as adept in preaching the word of God as they are in the sciences, like psychology and karate, the Spaniards brought us syphilis and the Catholic religion poisoned by pure communism. Sure they say the Spanish didn't go around killing off the Indians; on the contrary, they used to sleep with the Indian women and that's how our race was produced. But look at our color; no need to say it, if we were in the United States, they'd mistake us for blacks and we wouldn't be able to stay in hotels or ride buses with whites. What's more, they treat us worse than blacks because as for these, even though their color fucks them up, they're still considered Americans, while we latinos are neither here nor there with this nice little bullshit color of ours. It would have been better had

*we been either Indians or whites, without any in-betweens.
It's necessary to define oneself, brother. But the Spaniards
shit on us, even on our spirit, as I was saying; well, now it
turns out that the priests are even worse than the civilians,
and one has to go around figuring out how to put the brakes
on them, even if it means busting up those who are most
abusive. You saw what we did with the ones we've had to
get rid of. And the worst is that it makes us look bad, and
now comes the commie monsignor to excommunicate us.
And since the truth is that we're not really sure whether hell
exists or not, which is something we'll know only when we
kick the bucket, we're left to wondering if those bastards are
really sending us to the boilers. One can never be sure, right?
Even though the gringo tells us that the only true religion
is Christianity, their religion, and that priests have been
shitting on it ever since a Communist pope arrived on
the scene and they had to poison him which only goes to
show how much power they have. They've put in an anti-
Communist pope; they say he's among the worse, but even
so I have my doubts because Catholics are on their way to
Armageddon. Perhaps you don't believe me, brother, because they've been keeping you in the dark: the Communists
and the priests have already won you over. That's why one
has to sacrifice oneself by doing a number on so many poor
motherfuckers. The poorer they are, the more fucked up
they are. You know that already, don't you, brother? Before
this everything was fine and dandy, no one went around
stirring up trouble or even talking about things like a minimum wage. Why don't they just ask for the maximum wage
once and for all and skip all this bullshit? Imagine, now
they're even asking for cheese to eat. But Armageddon will
soon come to put an end to this entire race, unless we*

make a move to save ourselves. When in your blessed and motherfucking life did you ever have cheese to eat; it even gives one a stomachache when you eat anything but tortillas, salt and beans. But since so many sons of bitches inhabit this world, they come and enlist us to demand from the rich things that are beyond their means to give us. Look, brother, don't piss me off. If I'm fed up with the things I told you, it isn't so you'll criticize me. I have to eat well. That's why I didn't want to tell you anything. With me it's a question of work, and what's more, I belong to the armies of the Lord, because we're saving civilization not with perverse ideas out of books but through daily practice, relying on the resources of the most civilized nation in the world. Praise the Lord and pass the ammunition! Look, brother, if you want, we'll have one for the road and I'll pay, so you won't say I've changed for the worse. What happens is that you civilians think we're brutes and that we handle only weapons. But don't you see? We have our ideas, too. That's how we can be sure that no one is going to brainwash us.

Look, brother, don't chicken out on me. See, I've had twice as much to drink as you and it hasn't gone to my head, but you're already seeing little faggot angels. Don't blame me, and don't get yourself upset because you'll only have to calm yourself down. One more little beer, brother, as a chaser for the cane liquor.

You believe, brother. While I serve myself big, strong drinks, you pour little trickles for yourself.

You want me to hang one on so later you can say I can't hold my liquor, so you can damage my prestige. All right, brother, I promise you I won't insult you any more so have your beer.

Well, imagine, brother, as far as brainwashing is concerned, I tell the gringo: *Well, look, I thought that business about washing brains was pig soap and water.*

And everyone roared with laughter except the gringo, *who is a superserious person—he doesn't kid around with anyone.*

And he says to me: "You're right. It's like washing it with soap, any kind of soap, it doesn't matter. All that you understand about brainwashing, that's sufficient," he tells us. Because it's a very complicated scientific problem, it's not that simple, brother. And to be sure, we, because we're from a backward country, are ignorant. And we no longer ask anything. But my companions keep laughing. So the gringo *hollers, "Shut up, sons of bitches!" Because that name—you should hear how well he says it—it was among the first he learned, he told us one day, well, I think we're going to have to use it quite a lot. At that time we didn't understand what he meant. Soon after, we did, now that he calls us sons of bitches up and down. One day he explained that it was one of the norms of discipline. That we should start getting used to it and that we ourselves should learn how to use it when necessary in a natural manner.*

Because, look, once the gringo *gets pissed off, whoever stands in his way will bring down a storm, a shit storm. Believe me, it's something else, because from the beginning the director told us the* gringo *was authorized to do anything he wanted, like the Chinese man who eats "lice" and who can kick us in the ass when we can't make heads or tails of what he says. So you'll see that I'm sincere when I tell you that just as there are some things that we like there are other things that are hard to get used to at first.*

You don't mess with the gringo, *brother. Nor with the*

little Chinese man. They're here to make men out of us and to understand the problems of communism in this backward country. I'd like to see you getting a kick in the ass or a karate chop in the neck from the little Chinese man. Because if one begins to slack off in class or to fall even half asleep, hang it up. The Chinese man sneaks up from behind and pow! gives you a bitch of a whack on the neck. That's just to let you know that more than one have gone straight to the hospital and haven't returned. But that's the way it is, brother. What do you expect? What's worse is eating shit here, busting your ass from sunup to sundown for a wage that's barely sufficient to subsist on. What happens is that you were born to be a beast of burden, brother. They haven't even taught you to keep your mouth shut or else you wouldn't be telling me those things. And if I forgive you, it's because of your ignorance. But I can send you away from here all tied up, don't have any doubts about it; that's what I'm being trained to do by the Special Forces.

Even my mom and dad, even you, brother.

The thing is, all civilians are shit, brother; you're no exception. They envy our uniforms, the fact that we've gotten ahead in life.

That's why when it's time for us to take action, we don't spare anyone. Did you hear me, brother?

10 A. M.

It would be better if I were blowing on the fire. Making maté tea so as not to hear Pijiriche, so as not to hear him. He has been complaining to himself under the banana tree. A person's eyes can only take so much. One's heart, too. It's a pity, but he had it coming. What a time to have to piss! And what a place to choose!

"It's all right, I'm coming to get you." Because he hasn't wanted to come out from under the bushes. He's rubbing his wound against the dry banana leaves.

At last I've gotten away from that damned fire. And I say excuse me to the men, because even though it's your own home these people take over. So I won't provoke them needlessly. And I won't be rude, because it's true they won't even say hello; one should always show them good manners. Right? "That's what you get for being bad." And he wags his tail.

I come carrying my dog. "Poor little dog." And the man

still looks at me with a stone-faced expression as if a torrent of piss had fallen on his stinking leggings. The dog has been my companion for more than four years. How can we not be affectionate toward our animals. He's the children's plaything. He is their guardian. Their security blanket. The shadow that accompanies them.

And I go to the door almost without wanting to. To the door of sticks, to see if Adolfina is approaching with the children. Imagine her struggling with three little ones. And what's worse is that the littlest one does not like to walk. He almost can't, even though he does his best.

And I say:

—Soon she'll be appearing over there.

Talking to Pijiriche. I tell Pedro so Juan will hear. The truth is that she won't be arriving for a long time.

And again I say:

—They're about to come around the bend.

And they pretend not to understand. Well, they wait, wait and wait, they're patient because they're very sure of their authority. I would like nothing better than to relieve the tension. That way, when Adolfina arrives, everything will pass with no problem. They must want to verify something. Today one can't even keep up with so many calamities. Even innocent people find themselves in trouble. Adolfina is innocent. We're all innocent. The only ones at fault for the bad things that are happening are the authorities. They with their way of being. Their behavior. Yes, the only ones who go to jail or end up wounded or dead along the roads are the poor. And that's because the authorities have a predilection—they know who to hassle. They exist to boss the poor around. To order the poor about, to beat up on the poor and to carry them off as if they were animals. Someday the good life they're living will end. Always doing it to the people, always. They've never suffered the slightest hurt. That's where they get their pride from. Once they're in uniform they think they're kings of the world, and they themselves say they're disposed to anything. That's how it is. Why should I lie? All I'm doing is letting them be. Because I am so alone. But don't go believing that the torture of seeing them standing with their canteens, their machetes and their automatics doesn't take its toll on me. They even want to use our avocado-eating dogs as firewood. From these people there's no relief; but one of these days things are going to change. And José says that day is not far away. I don't know these things very well. I sympathize with those who get involved in things to secure our rights. And sometimes I participate a little; well, the truth is that José really does everything while I stay home with the children. It's hard for me to get out. But I tell them if I can be of any help. Within my possibilities. That's why we're here—to defend ourselves. Otherwise no one will. Each person should look out for his own interests. From that point of view I support those who belong to the federation of farmworkers.

—If she doesn't come quickly, we'll have to go get her.

Now I won't even explain anything to them. Well, why? If they're so dumb and don't understand that the child is coming with three kids and that she's not a little dove that can come flying.

They're speaking softly but I know they want me to hear them; they want to frighten me. The only thing I tell them is can I offer you something special. Don't get the idea that my granddaughter is an old lady. She's only fourteen; it just happens that she's well developed. When her time

101

came she just grew and put on some hips and became a graceful big woman. Her long hair, it almost reaches her knees. She has many things that are attractive about her.

Imagine, how can one permit oneself even to think that she'll be harmed. She is our blood. The blood of María Pía.

It's not a matter of being cowardly, not in the least. But so soon after the blood of my son was spilled, one feels fright in one's heart. I told myself: this is too much. I lost Justino; he knew why he joined the struggle. He used to talk to me about those things in a way that perhaps not even José can. So I told myself: forget this blood of my blood, even though I'd get a lump in my throat, even though I'd have to swallow my tears. But I'm not the one who's going to cry; I'm not going to give our enemies the satisfaction of seeing the least amount of salt fall from my eyes. They'll pay. That's what I told myself. Sooner or later. They'll pay. That's what I told myself. It's inhuman to do what those assassins did to my son. And no one who is a human being would do it. That's what I told myself.

With all this, how is it possible that they can wait under this same roof without accepting my hospitality, without accepting water from me? I offered them something one does not refuse: the sweet water that José has set aside, the pineapple drink. I want them to entertain themselves with something.

—Well, if you won't want some water, then maybe you'd like a few swigs of pineapple drink; but don't think it's contraband rum.

I laugh. I can be so foolish, for no other reason than to show my teeth. I'd rather that they wait for her here. She's going to get back late.

—It's pure refreshment and it's delicious.

How foolish one can be. Maybe deep down in my spirit I think I could soften their hearts. But may God keep me from thinking such things. When you give a gift, you shouldn't expect anything in return. In this, one must preserve one's integrity. I ought to keep them happy so they won't go searching for her.

And they say:

—Well, go ahead, that's your business.

The jars are brimming with sweet *chicha*. Extending his hand as if my offering were going to burn it. When the sergeant extends his hand, the private extends his. Very fearfully. These people are so distrustful. I know they wouldn't be able to turn down the *chicha*. It's too delicious.

—Well then, pass the *chicha*.

—Be careful it doesn't spill on your uniform, because it stains. It's pretty strong . . .

"Old hypocrite, she thinks she can buy us off with this shit," slowly lifting the ladle to his mouth.

—You, this stuff is delicious.

—That's how it seems, Sergeant.

Try it, don't be afraid, it won't make you drunk; it's pure pineapple. They were having a good time, drinking ladle after ladle of *chicha*. They finished the jar. *Chicha* doesn't inebriate but it's delicious. Even though it makes you a little dizzy.

Chepe Guardado has always told me that you must give drink to whoever is thirsty. The very first thing one offers a visitor is water. Especially here at the Kilometer and throughout Chalate. One feels like stripping, it's so hot.

Sometimes in the afternoon a breeze comes. It comes

from Honduras. Around four o'clock it starts going south. It is the south wind from Honduras. Nevertheless, between eleven, around eleven, and three, this place is a damn oven.

Chepe has offered me a *coyol* palm fan; it's good for cooling oneself and for fanning the fire.

For this reason, not just anyone will pass up a ladle of sweet pineapple drink seven days old, nice and fermented. Above all, I have used up Chepe's favorite drink so they'll forget about the child, won't get bored standing around. What's certain is that if they wanted to, they could go get her—she must not be more than a half-mile away; but it seems they don't want to budge.

All the better.

Luckily José isn't coming home for lunch. Thank God I don't have to think about it. I hope Chepe doesn't come home to sleep, as he did last night. It's better if he were to stay in the hills. As for me, I don't need a man in my bed. Only if it's chilly, you know.

MARIA ROMELIA

*My mother says that poor Guadalupe suffered a lot. It hasn't
even been three weeks. She threw on her shawl and her
semi-mourning that she wears on Sundays and hurried off
all discombobulated to where they had told her. You see,
they had found a person seriously wounded, way down the
hill, and everyone thinks it's Justino. "It can't be my son.
He's in Ilobasco working." And all at once we see her
tears. And the pounding of her heart was telling her yes,
it was him. Well, the truth is you couldn't even tell it was
him from his face. "People think it's him. I hope it's not
Justino; they must be saying so for a reason. I don't know
why the possibility of my son's death insinuated itself into
my heart." It was better to deceive her and tell her that
Justino was badly wounded; but the truth had already
spread, what they had done to Justino was something terrible: his body was found in one place and his head in
another, stuck on a road marker.*

And early in the morning, when people were going to work, that is, around six, they could see a ball elevated on a post. Well, who could think it had anything to do with a human being, in spite of so much current barbarity.

We saw how some people were running in the direction of Guadalupe's hut and we asked them what was happening and they told us and asked how to tell Doña Lupe without devastating her all at once. My mother told them to be very careful, it might be better if she were to see what happened with her own eyes. That way the blow won't be completely brutal. And it was necessary to let Chepe know at the plantation. Later, Lupe said she would go by herself so as not to frighten Chepe. "Let him work in peace. Take care of my children, sister." "Of course we will, sister Lupe." And she left with those who had come to tell her.

And people say:

—Imagine, I was working over there and I noticed that thing on the post, rammed onto the post, and I didn't pay any attention to it until someone stopped to look at it. And I had seen it for a few minutes; it caught my eye. You see, I get up very early to work and the darkness prevented me from seeing well. It wasn't that dark because there were already rays of sunlight, but I still couldn't make things out that clearly.

—A person dressed as a civilian had come to take him to his house. Justino's wife told me. She was in the yard and the children had gone to sleep in the hills with some friends, who had carried them on their backs because they're so little and they get tired. That's how she knew without seeing her. Well, Justino, for weeks, had been organizing the people of Chalate who were going to go to

the Bank. He had come from Ilobasco for that sole reason. At that time his wife thought it was about some infraction against the authorities that wasn't important. But, just in case, it was better not to let herself be seen. Besides, Justino had prepared her for something like this. "Let me go it alone, because it's better for the children to be orphans only of their father." She hid behind some coconut palm leaves they had collected days earlier to make a shower stall; you see, since many people pass along the road, they could easily be seen bathing and they couldn't do so in peace because people like to spy and are always tempted to look even if it's not out of malice—well, around here from five o'clock on people are on their way to work. "That's why I didn't do anything on Justino's behalf, and right away I was sorry; they didn't have him for more than three minutes when I heard a thud that penetrated my soul." With only one machete chop they did it. Look how they left all that I had. And now what will become of me?" They sliced his head off with one blow just when he turned his back to them. They didn't kill him from in front. At least he would have wanted that; he always faced others whenever he did them a good turn. A little later shots were heard.

—*He had more than seven bullet holes in him.*

—*And they say that those kind of bullets can cut down even a palm tree.*

—*So much bloodshed wasn't needed.*

—*And they say that when Doña Lupe reached the road where her son lay, she only shut her eyes . . .*

—*That she didn't shed a single tear . . .*

107

—*Anyone could say that it was hardness of heart, but if you know these people, you know it's not that . . . It's a way of gaining courage to live what remains of life.*
—*Yes, because the dead cease to suffer, but we the living must persist in this vale of tears.*
—*No one is going to doubt Lupe or Chepe, what with all the work they've done in this life, never making ends meet, never allowing themselves any luxury, only work and more work.*
—*It's hard to live as a daily wage earner.*
—*And she wasn't even able to pray for him on the ninth day . . .*
—*We can't get involved in someone else's pain.*
—*Not even the priest tried to intervene.*
—*José went back to work as usual and Lupe shut herself away for a few days.*
—*Sometimes I would go to my friend so she would lend me her children to take care of, but I never tried to raise the subject; what's the use of reliving . . .*
—*In cases like this one shouldn't even give condolences . . .*
—*No sharing the pain.*
—*Share life . . . that's what we ought to do.*
—*So these things won't happen anymore.*

Everything people say is a way of being with Lupe. To-day for you, tomorrow for me. We make her mourning our own.

The authorities didn't come around for a while, stopped showing up; whoever is at fault is afraid. Days without coming by.

They only came as far as the Detour, to drink their re-freshments at Don Sebastián's store.

As if there wasn't anything new under the sun. As if Don Sebastián were one of them. Or perhaps they'd talk just to talk. "Yes, everything is fine," *Don Sebastián would respond.* "That way they leave faster." *They stop hassling you so much.*

Now honest people are even afraid to go there. Because deep down inside no one wants any trouble with the authorities.

If one participates in things, it's not with the slightest intention of creating problems with the authorities.

A blow like that is very hard to withstand.

And people say:

—*I admire Lupe . . .*

—*How can she be so strong . . .?*

—*Don't you believe it; those blows weaken the body; that's why one grows old at an early age.*

That's what people keep saying.

And Chepe is made of no less sterner stuff. It happens that he is strong, is of the pure race; he must cry for his son inside his soul. He's as tough as a ceiba tree, and how he gets around, how he must suffer, how he worries about everyone else, not to mention his son. He never tires of trying to solve the problems of the community. We know the love he puts into things. He's the soul of the cooperative; he's here and there. What resilience! And, well, as for his humility, we also notice that he's different from others. For example, he won't allow us to call him Don Chepe. And he's such a prankster. He tells us himself when we're at the cooperative, "Just call me Chepe, none of this mister business with me." *And they say,* "Hey, Don Chepe, aren't you worried that children will lose respect for you?" *And he*

109

says, "I'm everyone's peer—if they come to the cooperative, they have the right to be peers regardless of age." And we got used to calling him José, or more affectionately, Chepe.

So we share his grief, even though we give our condolences to Lupe. He told us himself: "With me, no condolences, nothing about the ninth day. I'm going to ask the priest for forgiveness."

And the priest respected his way of coping with his grief for Justino.

We all respected it. "Life goes on," Chepe says.

10:30 A.M.

The dog is my brother.

The dog takes care of me nights when I'm alone with the children. And there's nothing but darkness enveloping me. The fear of not waking up the next day. Our reassurance is the dog snoring under the cart. The dog that sniffs around, barking from time to time at night.

There have been fifty generations of dogs since our Lord walked the earth accompanied by poor people. There they were trying to bite His tunic, playing, rolling around. The dogs of the Lord.

The dog is my son, my brother, my cousin, my uncle, my grandparents and my nephews, my granduncles, second cousins, my great-grandchildren and my great-great-grandchildren.

The dog barks to make his presence felt and he talks to me when he's hungry or when he's cold. The dog is like the chicks, except they don't sing songs about him at school.

Without a dog there's no family; that's the truth.

When the souls of the dead are up and about, it's better to tie the dog to a *jocote* or *madrecacao* tree because if you don't, they'll bite one another and the dog will get the worst of it. If he's tied up, things change because then the souls think he's a brother in suffering and they won't attack him. It must be a *jocote* or *madrecacao* tree.

My poor little dog that likes avocados. He lives off avocados that fall from the trees on coffee plantations. But I don't let him go hungry; I always throw him his own special tortilla. Pijiriche eats tortillas with salt like any of us, even though every now and then he goes outside in search of his own little things to eat and he'll probably eat avocados. I don't know.

There he is with his sad eyes, with eyes filled with tears, talking to me in another language that I don't understand.

"Signs for the intelligent and sticks for the dog," as the saying goes, but sometimes it works the other way, and the dog responds to signs, and the intelligent to sticks.

The dog is our master.

Pretty dog, soft hair, head like a gourd. Who hit him in the ribs? The guardsman.

Coffee-colored dog with sparkling eyes.

Dogs have mothers and fathers, even though at times they don't recognize either. But you have me, because you won't let anything happen to us; we are alive because of you, because you bite our enemies; you save us from our prowling enemies and from all evil.

Dog with tail cut off, wagging his stump to scare off imaginary flies. We cut off his tail with one machete blow when he was barely seven days old.

Red-brown and white dog, son of Tamagas and Gavilana; I mention this because I saw it with my very own eyes when they were all stuck together and couldn't be separated no matter how much water we threw on them.

Dogs have something of us in them. Something of God.

Dogs also go to heaven or to hell depending on what they deserve. They get rewards or punishments. That's the way it is with all animals friendly to man.

Dog, you make me suffer your anxieties when you run round and around your bed before lying down to rest.

Dogs bark at the darkness of the night.

What is the sixth sense that dogs have that allows them to smell danger a mile away?

At night they cry like newborn babies. In the distance dogs bark, and fear enters our bones because death is making its rounds.

We've always had two dogs, one that is always running about, and the other white with red and brownish spots. The one that used to run loose died, and we haven't wanted to replace him.

When a dog has rabies, you shouldn't strike him with a machete; one should tie a rope around his neck and hang him from a *tempisque* or mango tree. He suffers less and the rabies come flying out and won't contaminate anyone.

We have buried all the dogs that have died on us; we never leave them for buzzards to eat. In case they have souls, we won't fall into sin.

There are more dogs than people in the Kilometer. And in all of Chalate also.

The skinnier the dog, the more fleas will stick to him, because fleas have always been such sons of bitches.

A dog that barks will bite, that's something I have ample proof of: what happens is that when it starts to bite it stops barking. So it either barks or bites, one or the other.

When a dog barks, it's hungry.

Be careful of the dog that bites quietly.

Never chase dogs away because it's a sin. Dogs ought to be able to chase whomever they please.

My husband, my children, my brothers, my uncles, my cousins, my aunts, my grandparents and my parents. Then, my dog.

Dog's don't give rabies. One carries rabies within oneself and it can be released when the enmity of a dog and the blood of a man mix.

We call our worst enemies dogs, but they don't deserve it because dogs are the friends of man.

ADOLFINA

In the flash of an instant I thought about what I was going to say to them. I came upon these people on the road. It was them. With their weapons, their yellowish uniforms, the color of war. I came upon them just as I was going around the bend. They were sucking on sugar cane, peeling it with their machetes, talking among themselves, saying funny things because they were smiling. They smile when they think no one sees them. I was paying attention to the children and even carrying the smallest one piggyback and saying, "Hurry up, little girl, hurry up, little boy," but I saw them sucking on sugar cane, sturdy sugar cane.

No doubt they had snuck into someone's land and cut it. I saw them smiling. Laughing is a weakness for them and I caught them at it. In the end I pretended not to notice. Well, why should I care about the lives of these bandits.

My mother says I'm too rebellious, but my father has always told me one shouldn't call that rebelliousness but

*awareness. I'm unable to put up with those people called
the authorities. No matter how much I try. My mother tells
me they are doing their duty, that's what they're paid for.
That's not true. They don't pay them to kill. They're just
paid, and they do their job. "Then is their duty to kill?"
I ask my father.*

*"More or less," he answers. "Don't say those things to
the child, Helio," my mother says. And then, "They defend
the system, that's why they kill." And I tell him that that is
not good. "I didn't say it was good," he answers.*

*He tells me, "For as long as I can remember, the au-
thorities have been this way—they shoot first and ask questions later. Well, I began to understand," he continues.
"It's not just about getting annoyed or getting indignant."
I am also beginning to understand.*

*"It should be called awareness, not rebelliousness," he
tells my mother. My father always liked being in the organization; he was one of the first to join.*

*It's the only means for defending our interests; as a group
we are going to be stronger. That's how he'd talk to me. He
says he doesn't know how it came about that I was born so
smart. "Because a dummy I'm not, neither is María Pía, but
we're no great shakes; I barely passed the fifth grade; your
mother, yes, she finished elementary school." And he explains to me, "Poverty more than anything forces one to
clarify a lot about life, but I was never able to understand
a whole bunch of stuff."*

*My father is very frank. Now that he's old I've caught
on a little. I have begun to understand life, the origins of
our poverty. That's why I'm telling you, he tells me, "What
you've got isn't rebelliousness but awareness."*

116

*I love my father very much. I miss him a lot—we used to
talk so much. I sense that he likes to talk with me more than
with my mother; he likes to converse with me about things
whereas with my mother he talks less or only about ordinary
concerns. Such as the thickness of the tortillas or his belief
that eating only beans and corn makes us weak in the head,
even though they are nourishing; yes they are, but the body
tires of getting tortillas and beans for breakfast every day,
tortillas and beans for lunch, tortillas and beans for supper,
from your first cry when you leave your mother's womb
until your last breath.* "That's why I took care to give you
cheese when you were little, and if there wasn't any cheese,
then I'd look to see where I could get some." *And she continues telling me:* "And you, you were such a glutton, you
used to stuff yourself with cheese; you wouldn't eat unless
they'd serve you your little fresh cheese. No doubt that's
why you've turned out to be so bright, because that business
of intelligence has something to do with nutrition; you can
see why I believe that." *My papa is so handsome. I wonder
what they've done with him?*

"I would have been happy if you'd finished sixth grade
at least," *Mother says. And after thinking she continues:*
"Later we'll see what becomes of you; you have to take
advantage of your qualities." "We have to sacrifice ourselves for her, María Pía," *he tells my mother. She was here
with my grandmother Lupe when they told me:* "They took
your father away; you'd better not go back to Ilobasco."

*I miss him a lot, but the authorities won't let him go.
Why shouldn't I be offended by those criminals?*

*That he has never been here, they tell my mother that
they don't know anything, that a few days ago they let him*

117

go and that perhaps he doesn't love my mother anymore and went off with another woman.

All this foolishness they say to make fun of us, that's all. And it's hard to turn a deaf ear to such lies.

And to all these calamities are added new ones. I wonder how they knew I was around here in the Kilometer. From what Don Sebastián just finished telling me, "Well, it's funny, Adolfina, the authorities were here a little while ago and asked me about you. I told them you are the grand-daughter of Chepe Guardado, a child, in case there was some mistake." "I hope I haven't stuck my foot into it," I tell him.

—*It's her business.*

—*She comes from time to time to see her grandmother Lupe; she's not from around these parts, she lives in Ilobasco.*

"What I wanted was to defend you," Don Sebastián tells me.

—*Which is Lupe's house?*

"And they went in that direction, they must have run into you." "Yes, they were chewing sugar cane as they walked, but they didn't pay any attention to me," I tell Don Sebas. "They don't know you personally; well, they were very quick to ask if I knew you." "My grandmother is alone, and how will I get there from here with these children?"

—*Does she come here often?*

—*Once a year, perhaps, Sergeant.*

—*Let's go to her house.*

"And I try to explain to them that I don't even know if you were around here." On certain Sundays she comes," I say just to bullshit them. "But not always."

—We'll go that way slowly.

I have to go quickly, please hurry up. I wonder what this is all about. And he gives one piece of candy to each of the children, the three-for-five kind. "It must be just a routine matter," *he tells me.* "I have to go by for the tortillas."

—My grandmother Lupe is alone.

"Luckily, it doesn't have anything to do with her, nor with Chepe, and since you are a child they must respect you," *he tells me.* "We'll see," *I say.*

Because with the authorities one can never be sure.

At that moment a little woman from the neighborhood arrives at the store.

"Doña Lupe sends word that you shouldn't tarry on the way home because the butchers are asking about you." *And she says to be very careful that you show them enough respect, because she wouldn't want to have any trouble.*

Ah, my grandmother. I think. What happened to my uncle Justino is making her nervous. And because of that we decided not to tell her about my father, who was being held prisoner.

—And what else did she tell you?

—To bring some cheap tomatoes for tomorrow's rice. To-day's rice turned out as white as a hospital.

Look what a good little girl for running errands, I think.

"Down over there they've left their jeeps, two of them, but I only saw a pair heading toward Lupe's," *Don Sebastián tells me.*

I think: He who has done nothing has nothing to fear.

119

—*Don't squeeze them so much, because if you do I'll have to eat them myself.*

—*Ah, Don Sebastián, just because I touched them. Give me ten cents' worth of those that are ripest, then.*

—*Yes, take the ones that are nice and ripe because Lupe always likes tomatoes that are a little past their time.*

—*You just want me to take ones that are beginning to rot.*

—*Lupe was certainly right when she said that you're argumentative, little girl.*

—*Ay, how Don Sebastián does carry on.*

—*Just look at this little sign.*

I look at the sign written on the wrapping paper: "If you're not buying me, don't handle me."

—*Well, that doesn't have anything to do with me, Don Sebastián, because I'm going to buy, so give me these ripe ones.*

—*And hurry up, little lady, so I can see what those people want.*

—*Well, I'm not going to hurry to satisfy someone's caprice, especially since I have these children with me. If I do, it's for Lupe, she must be worried, you should see how we all worry about her, after what happened to Justino she hasn't been the same.*

Deep within, my heart skips a beat. There's also the business with my father, but Don Sebastián doesn't know anything about it. May God's will be done.

"Hurry up, kids!" And I go along pulling lizards off the tihuilote trees. "If you don't hide, I'll tear your head off." But the lizard moves quickly, tricking me by changing its color from stripes to paye gray. I like it when their tails come off and the little tails start flopping around. They say that later the lizards return and they glue their tails on with

*their own saliva. Like iguanas, no matter how many times
you pull off their tails, you never see one without a tail.*

"Pull that one down," *I say to my uncle Benjamin. To
think that these children are my uncles. And Moncho is
only two years old. My uncle Moncho. My aunt Ester, four.*
"Hurry up, kids! Let's go, my uncle and aunts!" *Poor little
things.*

With the sun as hot as it is. "Walk in the shade, you're
going to burn your feet." *They're used to walking where it's
hot now.*

The shade of the tihuilote *trees.*

"Walk on the grass."

At the same time the cicadas begin to buzz. "They say
they are crying for Christ." *My grandmother must be
worried.*

*The cicadas buzz because the sun is strong. It's a way
to protest the summer. Their concert is heard all over the
hills. The music of the cicadas. Like the horn of a pickup
truck: chiquirun-chiquirin, ting-a-ling. Everywhere.*

*If one is looking for the cicadas, they're in the branches
of* tihuilotes, *pissing on people who are seeking shade underneath. I tell the children that we should move into the
shade, the ground is hot.*

The weeping of cicadas saddens me.

Maybe because of Holy Week.

*The same thing happens to everyone. One shouldn't run
during Holy Week because that's kicking Christ. One
shouldn't spit because that's spitting at Christ. They say
that only nonbelievers spit. And if one throws a stone, already you're stoning Christ; even if it's only a lizard that
you hit, in truth the one you're really hitting is Christ.*

These are things we're taught from childhood. My mother

doesn't believe much of it, but my grandmother still believes in those things. Everyone pretends to believe. "It's the Christian faith," says grandmother.

The sound of the cicadas heralds the advent of Holy Week. That's why it makes you melancholy. Not me. Just a little, that's all, because people are like that. Even though one might not want to. One accepts it as true. We all accept it as true. Some more than others.

Perhaps it isn't even important.

"Uncle Benjamin, move into the shade." "But the cicadas will piss on me," he says. "That's all right. Worse if it were to give you the pissing sickness."

And he comes over under the tihuilotes.

"Carry me piggyback, Aunt Adolfina," Moncho tells me. In his own way of speaking. Have patience, we're about to reach the bend. And he begins to cry. "Aunt Ester, hold the tomatoes for me so I can take care of Moncho. It's only a little farther. I told you all that you shouldn't come." From the bend one can suddenly see the door of the house. Around here I buy tortillas.

It's so hot.

Uncle Moncho has stopped crying, poor thing; he walked more than enough for his age.

The little bandit fell asleep. His little head on my shoulder. His little head is covered with sweat as if he were sick.

Sleep, my love.

I enter the house of María Romelia. "Good morning."

11:30 A. M.

A cloud is wrestling with the sun. Like dogs and cats, the clouds and the rays of the sun. The cloud of dust is a haze; it won't let you see beyond. The match is won by the sun and everything calms down. Now comes a clear breeze, bathed with fresh homemade soap. A wind that makes you want to breathe it all in until there's no more left. "The wind is a little prankster that carries my notebook, carries my bag" is the only song I learned at school. I got as far as second grade. I sort of learned to read and write, but I never used a book bag; well, I only had a five-cent notebook and a pencil. I learned to read in Our Lady of Magnificence by means of prayers: to Santa Lucía, Our Fathers, I a sinner, and the Creed, you learned to read in those days at the top of your lungs. If you didn't have the lesson memorized you couldn't leave school, and not only that but they made you kneel to read. The most common punishment was kneeling or holding one's hands above one's head in imitation of the *anima sola*. The instruction was severe, but one learned. What happens as time passes is that one starts to forget everything. You see, there's no need for us to read, so we start becoming dunces slowly but surely.

The sergeant scratches his leg. I say he's a sergeant because of the little red stripe there. Maybe a flea that Pijiriche threw his way as revenge. Maybe he's left his mind in town, because he must come from a town like ours, or probably a little larger. He presses his thumb, the nail of his thumb, against the thick cloth of his uniform, the color of cow shit. All that remains is for him to get desperate, and to begin spouting proclamations on his own. And when the authorities insult themselves, it's a sign of impending grief—one will have to bear the brunt. That's the way it's always been. That's why people say: As to the authorities, keep them content. And there goes a little chicken, and here are a few eggs, these small bananas, this can of corn. That's life.

I see them through the screen of sticks. Both of them. Only one of them has to do with the flea, the sergeant. He makes himself comfortable on a branch of the fruit tree. He keeps pressing his thumbnail into the thick cloth without being able to relieve the itch. "A fucking flea from that fleabitten dog."

The other guardsman yawns, and all bunched up he traces figures on the ground with a stick, and then he looks at something. I look, too. It's an ant with a little green leaf on its back. The private picks up the ant by the leaf. It holds on to the leaf. He holds it close to his eyes. "Crazy ant; these little bastards are so fucking strong." And he squashes it between his fingers. The little green leaf comes loose and

falls as if flying, as if it didn't want to fall. And I go to
the cooking fire again. Adolfina should be arriving soon. I
feel like going out and looking for her, but what for. They'll
say no; I'd better not waste my breath.

I speak. To no one. To myself. "Ain't life a drag?"

The sergeant looks at me. Maybe they had forgotten
about me. A silence of mad dogs. So much solitude is
making me afraid. I wish I had a visitor right now. I don't
know what would happen. But they would come to save
me. If even my neighbor were to show up. But no. Why
wish trouble on a neighbor who doesn't deserve any. One
must respect the guardsmen's silence.

And I ask myself: "Why haven't the children come yet?"

Once again there's the dog-and-cat fight between the
sun and the clouds. It would be nice if the clouds were to
win so that the children could walk without burning their
feet. The sky begins to get overcast. Again the wind blows.
Cool wind like water in earthen jars. I shiver, as if I were
cold. It's a miracle when it gets cold here at this time of day.
We call it the devil's hour because only he would dare to
venture out and take the sun away. He's such a glutton for
punishment.

—One must be ready for anything.

—. . .

—This old bitch is giving me the jitters.

—Or maybe it's that dog. I'd love to pump a bullet into
   him if it weren't for the racket it would cause.

"That's what they're trained for, Lupe; they defend a
system." If it weren't for José, I'd be dead by now. "You
have to understand and then you'll see how the problems
are solved in another way—not by the will of one person, I

125

like that or I don't like that. As to whether they're wicked? No, Lupe, they're not wicked, they're not sons of bitches, they're just like any one of us, except that they're in the enemy camp; they themselves, are in their own enemies' camp. You'll never see one of the authorities owning a plantation, a two-story house or a luxury car; they barely get to drive around in a jeep that is an instrument of labor, like a machete is to us. You won't see them wearing fine clothes. No, when they're in civilian clothes they look as humble as we do, you can't even recognize them; they become different people from what they are when they go visit their children and their mother and their father. It's not a fabrication of mine or of others, this is as clear as day." That's what he tells me.

Without José we would be lost. "That's why the problems can't be solved by a single person, but only by all of us working together, the humble. The clearheaded ones. And this is very important: you can be humble and live in darkness. Well, the thing is not a matter of being or not being humble. The problem lies in our awareness. The awareness we will have. Then life will become as clear as spring water." Where would I be without José?

"You shouldn't forget that this uniform defends itself to the death, our lives are explained by this rifle; we're powerful and they'll fear us as long as we know when to grab it like men and shoot when we think it's necessary. As long as our hands don't tremble we're saved." "That fucking flea continues to bite me."

—It looks like the child is coming over there.

—I think you're right . . .

—Get up, then, don't just sit there.

Pijiriche takes off. Happy. His stub of a tail wagging.

I'm happy. They have remained calm: one trying to get at the flea and the other watching the ants. This little girl has taken so much time that it's a miracle the men have not gone looking for her. And the worst is that no doubt she hasn't yet entered my neighbor's house to buy tortillas.

That is to say, these men may get violent when they figure out that she isn't coming. I saw the glee in their eyes when they thought they saw someone by the ridge. "There! It looks like a child is coming." And at that moment she was probably entering my neighbor's house. "Good morning." And she'll probably have to wait a long time. Well, these people could tell me what they want and I'd take care of it in a hurry; but they've gotten mysterious about the child. That's what worries me.

—What's happened to the kid, eh?

—She probably slipped away.

—I thought they were coming over there, by the bend.

—If you only knew how bored I am.

And I can't do anything but play the crazy old woman. If they want to talk to her, well, let them wait. Nothing can happen to a child.

THEM

Well, look, all these women are whores; to be a woman is to have been born a whore, while men are separated into two types: the faggots and we the machos, who dress in this uniform. And among the machos one could even select the most macho: those of the Special Forces, those of us who have gone to school with Chinese karate experts and gringo psychologists. Those of us who eat mashed potatoes to be strong. We cannot be complacent with our enemies; we must be tough as steel, unyielding. We're not unyielding. We're not like Nicaraguans, who only know how to kill, but who don't have the right attitude toward civilians, who eat with them, allow themselves to be invited to things, nothing but lack of self-respect; being congenial is queer business. Nor are we like Hondurans, who accept into their ranks even the lowest scum and that's the reason they are always talking about divisions among the ranks, of nationalism. We're different, we're together. United unto death, and we don't go around giving civilians any benefit of the doubt, God help us, because if you give a hand to a Salvadoran he'll take an arm; if you laugh with him, he'll think you're a whore or a faggot. So no half-ass measures with civilians. It's like shrimp fishing: if you fall asleep, the currents will take them away. And here's another thing, the Salvadoran has a predilection for communism, ever since 1932.

So how then are we going to be nationalists, if nationalism says we're all equal? And the truth is that we're not equal to the rest of the people, none of that here. Well, how are we going to be the equals of civilians who have strong inclinations toward communism? We prefer what's foreign because what comes from abroad doesn't come to fuck us up but almost always to do us good. While the Salvadoran, by virtue of being Salvadoran, thinks he has the right even to shit on you. So we cut off their water; and if we have to kill, we'll kill the Salvadoran because the Salvadoran has one notorious characteristic: that of being a son of a bitch. It's not that I want to shit on my people, rather it's the truth and Christ died for the truth. The day a Salvadoran civilian gets to be president of the republic, you can forget it, because they'll hang us all by the balls. And it isn't necessary for the gringo of the Special Forces to emphasize this; we know it ourselves. Because what's important, the gringo tells us, is not for you to be here for the money or for the good food you get, but out of conviction; you are the soldiers of God, the saviors of this damned country that loves communism so much.

No sooner had the Communists triumphed in 1932 than they began to ravage the people, the rich, because hatred here is for the rich. We're born with envy inside us; we can't look at someone with joy and satisfaction in our eyes

*because we're already thinking how we'll shit on him. And
we exist precisely to stamp out all forms of envy. Exterminate it at gunpoint with decisiveness, firmness. We're
getting more and more prepared because communism is
almost here. Our foreign teachers don't let down for a
minute. They say they're willing to die with us for freedom
and democracy; to wipe away all traces of nationalism. I
agree with all of this: as for the race, it must be exterminated by fire. All those perversions are going to end when
we are all united in Christ, when we all embrace Christ,
destroy the Communist priests. Don't think we have some
kind of religion other than the true one, the other, that
comes from above; they allow us to choose Latter-Day
Saints, Mormons or the Children of Faith, because these
religions bring light and hope for the eternal happiness of
man.*

*So we can't go around respecting that business about
brothers, uncles, cousins, and even mothers and fathers. If
they want to remain in the dark, that has nothing to do with
me—to each his own. Whoever wants to turn his backside
into a drum, let him. And if bullets are what they want,
well, leave them in their stupidity, because they'll get them
in flurries. We can't be concerned with philosophical questions, much less with sentimentality.*

*As for women, the older they get, the more whorish. It's
true. Everything's clear, but some have doubts, especially
because of their mothers. But the* gringo *makes it clear:
"That is to say, those who at any given moment resist or
present an obstacle to the security of the country." To be
sure, there are exceptions, but they're very few. For example,
I don't believe that my mother is a whore nor will she ever
be one; you see, I'm going to teach her not to lean toward*

the enemy camp. *Our trainers tell us: "You all have to help to make your families see the light." Of course, one can't start wasting time with them; just because they're your family that's not to say they're not dumb. Even I have some cousins off somewhere getting involved in stupid shit. I've already warned them, indirectly, so as not to get in trouble with my parents. You see, the truth is that they're still in the dark, although I'm not going to tell the instructors; they wouldn't understand. It's not because I'm afraid.*

But, for example, even my sisters are nothing different. They, like all women, have been going around searching for husbands from when they were little; I mean, even at fifteen they were hankering to go off with someone. That's why there's so much misery in this country, because as the women are whores they don't waste any time in having children. If you don't believe that women are most responsible for all this misery, imagine, there are more than five million of us on this little piece of earth, and they want us to redistribute the land. Imagine, what kind of share would each of us get? Barely a spot to stand on, just big enough for your feet. I'm not saying they're dumb. There isn't even space enough for graves. Because it's only right that if the land is going to be divided, it should be done fairly and each person should get an equal share. If not, they really have got to stop walking around talking all that shit.

And one's sisters, as soon as their men get bored with them, there they are returning to their parents so these grandparents must take care of a litter of kids they're now stuck with. Didn't I tell you they were sly whores? That's why if there's ever to be a little tranquillity around here, that is to say, when there aren't so many agitators because we've exterminated them all, it's not that our work will be done, it'll only be of another kind: for example, carrying out family planning campaigns, enforcing birth-control programs. That'll be our future mission. Our country will be great only when it is inhabited by sons and daughters who love and respect and are willing to die for it.

As for religion, we'll have our work cut out for us, too, convincing people to embrace Christ. We've got to uproot everything. Because in 1990, when He comes to earth, as it's been announced, only those of us who are with Christ will be saved. Because He's coming to punish everyone, except His own. Everyone is going to be fried to a crisp. Except those of us who are Children of Faith.

And what's more, He might come early. Might change the date of His arrival. That's why our mission must proceed as quickly as possible, that's why we must act boldly, decisively and firmly.

No second thoughts. That you're my friend or my godfather or my brother. That's all bullshit. Either we are or we aren't. The rest isn't worth diddly-squat.

In reality I'm not such a brute. My favorite class is sociology; I'm a little weak in karate. But that's the way it goes.

What saved me was the fact that I was good in social studies and finished the sixth grade and that was how I was selected for the Special Forces.

This is how I've risen. My family is poor. What happened is, my brothers and sisters couldn't study. They preferred working to studying; already when they were seven years old they were going to pick coffee, cotton and cacao. That's the decisive age: you either go to school or to work. I began working at seven, but then they sent me to school and the teacher said I had promise and that they ought to

*send me even if only every now and then. What I went
through to finish the sixth grade! But look at me now. Here
I am. No one is going to take away what cost me so much.*

*And then I went to San Salvador and lived there until I
became a success. Well, my sisters also came to San Salvador, but because they were loaded down with kids they took
them to my parents and dumped them off and then came
back, but imagine for what! And there's no end to this. I
hear that two of them have been seen on Independence
Avenue, where the bad women live. So, let them sell their
bodies. It used to make me feel ashamed to admit it, but not
anymore, because our* gringo *instructor who is also a minister, a religious and karate teacher, told us that that's
what's good about democracy: everyone can do whatever
they want, there's individual freedom.*

*There are injustices as well. We should be honorable
enough to recognize them. But democracy is that way. The
business about equality of all: bullshit. The world has pro-
gressed precisely because we're not all equal. Imagine, how
am I ever going to be the equal of the little Chinese man?
He's the karate expert, not me. How is my sister ever going
to be the equal of those girls who mount horses in those
horseback-riding competitions? That's idiotic. God created
us all equal but different from each other.*

*I remember when I used to go with my entire family to
pick cotton. We would take even the smallest one, who was
only seven years old. With her hat for the sun and a bag full
of food and mats to sleep on. All of us picking while the
foreman took down our names. We, the children, weren't
put on the list because that meant you had a right to tortillas
and beans, and they weren't about to feed all of us, only the
adults. But we carried our salt with us in order to eat our*

*fill of tortillas and salt. And water, we used to carry water
in gourds.*

*And no one died of hunger. Well, two of my brothers
died, but it was because of my mother's carelessness. When
they got diarrhea, she didn't act fast enough and they died
of dysentery and dehydration.*

*Almost all children in rural areas die that way. Maybe
because of our ignorance, which makes us procrastinate,
then go to the drugstore when it's already too late. And as
there are no doctors. . .*

But a whore is a whore.

*And the instructor tells us: "About that uniform, respect
it. You have to respect it even when you're lying with a
woman." And then some wise guy tells the* gringo: *"You
see, it's like when you're lying with a woman, you're not
wearing any uniform or anything else. And as if that wasn't
bad enough: lack of respect for the minister!" Snickers.
Then the* gringo *grabbed an eraser with a wooden handle
and threw it at the wise guy's face. Right in the eye! Off
to the infirmary. As a Jehovah's Witness he's all right, but
as a military instructor he does not bullshit.*

*In other words, it's not all fun and games. This uniform
is my life. It has caused me to sweat blood.*

*Get this, the other day someone let go a loud fart. When
we were in bed. There was an explosion of laughter. The
sharp ears of the* gringo *who was writing at the other end
of the barracks heard either the unlucky fart or the
laughter. We were all quiet when he opened the door and
the light hit us. He didn't say anything; he turned and went
outside into the garden. Our barracks has only a roof, no
walls, so that we'll get used to living outdoors. Well, guess
what he was doing: he connected a hose to the faucet and*

hosed us down. That night we couldn't sleep because it was cold, and the sheets and mattresses were so wet and cold that even the shit in us froze.

He told us: "That's for fooling around." So, you see what I mean?

Big zero. Although I very much respect him as a spiritual guide. And there are things about our training I can't talk about because they're secret.

That is, this uniform you see me wearing so proudly isn't so easy to wear; it's not for everyone.

And then they go around blackening our reputation, saying that we have it easy, that all we do is persecute people. What you don't know you shouldn't say shit about. Enemies of the nation. Because an honorable person wouldn't go around talking through his asshole.

11:45 A. M.

I don't know why at this moment you come to mind. You're probably keeping me company as you promised when you were little. It would be better if you didn't come; well, you could die twice. Though you haven't died even once. It would be better. Things are as bad as they can get; if you want to come, then come. Because for a long time now you've been my little Saint Anthony, my magnificent, my talisman, all the things that one believed in in life.

Until you appeared.

And you found your father ready. Your mother was less in favor, but she understands where things are headed. Where José and Justino are, there I will be, my son.

Where your son dies you also find yourself. That's why I stood on the dusty road. I felt you didn't flinch even when you saw the machete about to chop your neck off.

I was watching. There wasn't a frown on your face. You knew we would all be watching. You wouldn't set a bad example for us. And if you didn't resist, it was because they took you by surprise, when in the twilight of dawn you were getting ready to leave the house.

And if now I offered them a little water or some pineapple *chicha*, I did it only because giving drink to the thirsty is the most sacred thing in life. You can't deny that even to the most wicked of people. There was not a drop of hypocrisy or servility in my offer. It's a matter of offering what not even God would deny the devil. You must understand, Justino. No one is giving her heart to these evil men and murderers. You would do the same thing, and not out of cowardice or treachery or resignation.

"When I die," you once told me, "I'm going to come and pull your leg. I'll appear, not suddenly because I wouldn't want to scare you, no, I'll greet you face to face: 'Good morning, Mama,' " and that would be enough. Well, you weren't really going to pull my leg.

But you never came openly. Only your shadow.

Even now I can feel your body. As if your breathing were suffusing all the corners of the house. You fill the house with your odor of balsam.

You have brought fresh air.

The songs of the mockingbird, of the wren and the dove have accompanied you. As if you had walked through the house on tiptoe.

"So you belong to the organization, you son of a bitch! Why doesn't it come to defend you now? Where's the courage of your organization now? So you're the one who's going to bury the landowners? Tell us where you got the gun. Asshole, tell us who gave it to you regardless of the fact that we're going to kill you. If you tell us, we'll do it quickly; if you don't, no doubt about it, we'll kill you

137

slowly so that you'll suffer. Tell your federation of peasants to come save you! You see, with the authorities you don't fuck around; we are going to kill everyone.

And as you weren't telling them anything, they found your silence insupportable. In essence you shit on them, because they would have wanted to make you suffer, to torture you slowly. But they couldn't take it; for them silence is the worst offense. Something unforgivable. The worst offense is not to be afraid of them, to maintain composure even when they're beating you with their rifle butts. The enemies of the people.

Then the machete appeared. The only road open to you, guardsmen, is drenched with blood. For all of you, life has no meaning, only death. And when you go around messing people over, you reek of death, the odor of cypress sticks to you.

You walk with a cemetery full of crosses on your backs, and you don't even notice, a ceaseless terror that you convert into aggression. But in spite all of this, I can still offer you a little water.

A sip of pineapple *chicha*. You mustn't consider it an act of kindness, nor of commiseration. It's simply a human act.

With your daily killings, you'll know when you live again, you'll see, you'll see. And you'll probably be able to laugh with us. Join us in eating a piece of tortilla and salt. We'll exchange nice and affectionate words. All it takes is being born again.

You all should live.

I tell them this, Justino, so that you'll also hear. Because I know you're here, and as you're shy you don't want to appear. You don't want to say anything as if the cat's got your tongue. Because I know: you come around here every day, you drink your fill of water and you leave quietly so as not to frighten me. You come only to see how we're doing. To say, "Hi, how are you," without saying it directly. I know.

I know because I leave a trail of ashes near the water gourd when I go to the yard or while I'm asleep and later I find prints there, your barefoot prints; so as not to make even the slightest noise you take your shoes off. I know the shape of your feet. And I also know how you smell after work: it's like the odor of balsam. Nothing but your shadow. It suffices for us to thank you for worrying about us. Your silent "Hi, how are you" and your invisible body. We don't see you, but we sense your presence, Justino. That's enough.

11:50 A. M.

I like to reminisce. It is the voice of conscience that used
to talk to them. "It's because you walk with your mouth
open," my mother would tell me when I accompanied her
and stumbled. Or when I was reviewing my primer and
she'd explain to me, "My papa loves me. I love my papa.
'Pa-pe-pi-po-pu.' The *guayaba* of Peru, tell me just how old
are you."

And I would go into the streets to catch butterflies.

I didn't like going to school because it was so far away,
more than a couple of miles. I preferred to help my mother
make tortillas. "You have to learn to read," she would tell
me. Or I would prefer to go with her when she went to pick
cotton on a nearby plantation. Wearing a big broad-brimmed
hat; one doesn't get much sun harvesting coffee.

I, who was only seven years old, found the work very
tiring but I preferred it to repeating "My dog is called Fido"
or "Fido, bring the ball to your master" or "Fido-fufo-faro-

foca-fumo." Fofofofó who farted, fofofofó who farted. By licking your fingertips and assigning them the names of the possible culprits you could tell who was guilty: the finger that dried first.

A most lovely morning to go to the river. "Will you give me permission to go bathing in the river with my little girl friends?" "How could you think such a thing? You're so bad, don't you know that little girls shouldn't go out alone? I'll give you a swat if you don't stop misbehaving." "Maruca has a doll." "Zape, bad cat! Go to your house." Books were always being written differently from how one spoke.

I ended up not going to school. And my mama said it was bad to live in ignorance because that way it was easier for them to cheat you; you'd be more at the mercy of intelligent people. "What's this business of spending so much time with your father?" Because I loved my father very much, I would always stick close to him. Because the teacher was real mean and if it rained a lot I could be dragged by the current to the sea. And that was for sure. In the rainy season it was dangerous, especially because one had to cross a brook where the currents are dangerous.

"Well, you know what you're doing," my mother would say. Already by six o'clock in the morning I'd be with my father winding up rolls of string. You see, that was his livelihood: he'd buy *mezcal* fiber and make twine, which he would sell in town, at a fireworks store that used to pay him a good price. My papa would walk backwards while I spun the spool and the twine would be wound; it would get longer and longer and he'd look small because he was more than fifty yards away making the twine. I had even gotten very muscular in the arms and was strong enough to lift bags of corn. My mother used to admire my strength.

"As a result of being with your father so much, you're starting to do the work of mules instead of helping me shell the corn." Or knead tortillas or wash clothes or cook beans and corn.

How I used to like coming home, tired, sweaty, happy about doing what I liked. My father, carrying balls of twine on his back, looked like a coconut tree, with coconuts on his back. And I with the spool: "Wait for me, Papa." Well, I earned my daily bread from an early age. "Hurry up, child, it's almost noon." Following him, noticing there were no shadows; you see, that's the sign that it's noon, when you can't see your shadow because the sun is directly overhead, at its peak in the sky.

When I was a little bigger, all of us would go to the coast to pick cotton. I always liked to stare at things with my mouth open. For example, in front of the sea, seeing it fall from the sky, seeing the great white bulls appear above us, looking at the horizon from the beach, looking at the sunrise. My teacher used to say that sea water goes up, in vapors. And then that same water falls as rain. I used to think about all these things as I picked cotton, wearing my wide-brimmed hat, and later I'd tell my father let's go down to the beach to look for shells. And he used to enjoy catching crabs. And at other times we'd catch shellfish, which we'd sell to people passing by in cars to the beaches.

In other words the water rises to the sky by means of invisible rivers, and that's why huge showers of rain fall in the winter. There are powerful storms that bring even frogs and snakes with them. I used to think this was not possible, but if you consider that water rises from the earth, then yes, it could be possible. We used to spend two months on the coast. Sometimes three. Big parties when we'd return, prayers to the Virgin of Perpetual Succor to protect us and allow us to return in health and peacefully.

On the same day of our return we would go to swim in the river. All morning long. We would watch the little dragonflies as they hit the water, you can almost hear them going chucumblum, trying to catch mosquito larvae swimming on the surface. And we screaming, as we tried to kill the dragonflies with sticks. "How sinful. Put down those sticks. And be careful not to touch a dragonfly or you'll wake up with your eyes stuck together," that's what she used to shout at us while she washed and watched us so that we wouldn't get near the well; you see, there was a whirlpool that could suck us right in.

And it used to get cold. We would dry ourselves in the sun. It is by means of the sun that children who die rise to the sky. It's not that angels can fly because they have wings, but because they can float in the atmosphere, which is full of solid things, one of which are the invisible rivers. Little angels don't exist. Children don't suffer when they die. When they're dying, yes. And upon their last breath, right there the body is separated from the soul. Only the body is ravaged by worms. Maybe these beliefs will always exist; well, hope remains alive, even if someone you love dies. Maybe the spirit is the memory that gets into your head. Because regardless of how much time passes, one cannot forget one's loved ones. The saying "Out of sight, out of mind" doesn't work in practice. We all suffer an eternity when someone disappears. And even more if it is your own child. Your own blood. There is a laceration, a pain that one feels; the heart is torn apart.

Only a mother can know that laceration. No one forgets his pain, that's a lie. It's buried there in memory and remains inside you forever.

I love the vapor of water, taking into account that it is the river in which spirits navigate, the river in which angels who were children float. My father would tell me that one should believe in these things, because that's the only way that life has meaning.

And it was because I walked around thinking a lot that my mother would call me "big mouth."

Later, Chepe opened my eyes—those things don't exist. I believe everything he says. Well, he's always right; nonetheless, there's a little light in one that tells you not to believe or to believe.

Until someone clarifies these things for us.

As for my father, don't mention him: he believed in the goblin, the *Cipitio*, the *Siguanaba*, the *Cadejos*.

And it wasn't just a matter of believing; they'd also appeared before him. Since he was a bit of a flirt, these things appeared to him as a kind of punishment. He would tell me about them when we were rolling twine or when we were shelling corn. Maybe his purpose was to scare me. Sometimes I couldn' even sleep as I was thinking about the *Siguanaba*. I would imagine it just as my father described it. Or as Chepe told me, "You won't believe how funny he was."

I don't know why we have to live off such fears. The little light of hope that lives in you, maybe.

The unknown always prompts us to seek the truth.

The reason must have something to do with that.

Those mysteries facilitate life, but so do real things: rice, when it's available; corn to make tortillas; salt so that food won't be tasteless, and for tortillas when one runs out of everything. And finally hope. We poor people can't live without taking these things into account. Neither more nor less. We think more than we should about hope. Like the light of a candle, it is. We would not be able to see in the darkness. A little later José began to tell me: hope is the sustenance of fools. I had never believed him. I understand what he's getting at, but I don't take him literally. Hope also nourishes us. Not the hope of fools. The other kind. Hope, when everything is clear. Awareness.

I remember the trips to the river. To catch little frogs by hand and to kill tiny river horses so as to put them into glass jars. I think more than I should. To think is nice. Since we have limpid minds, thought comes clearly, in big spurts. Especially if I am by myself with the children. If Adolfina comes, I think less, maybe because I look at her more. This way, my time passes. Looking at her. She's the living image of my daughter María Pía. She looks a lot like her mother.

ADOLFINA CONVERSES
IN THE CATHEDRAL

Today we went to occupy the Cathedral in San Salvador. It all began with the death of my uncle Justino Guardado, a few days after the demonstration at the Bank. On the road to Ilobasco where he had his house. One night, four members of the civil authority, those who are armed, went to his house, they dragged him out under a shower of blows and decapitated him, they dragged his wife and children out, and set fire to the house. My uncle Justino.

Who knows where they took him. The next day his body was found beaten and beheaded. His head stuck on a jiote post, those that are used to mark off property. The rest of his body was thrown in a ditch nearby.

The whole town was outraged, without knowing what to do because we all loved Justino and he did not deserve to die that way—he was a hard worker and a good son, one of the mainstays of his family and of my grandmother Lupe. He always helped her with her little chores.

But the four who took him away were well known in the region. Then the men of the region got together.

"Justino's hands were never stained with blood. He was a good man."

"All Justino did was help organize the demonstration at the Bank to demand a discount on seeds and fertilizer. That's all."

"So what are we going to do in memory of our companion?"

And a group was formed to find the murderers. Armed with clubs and machetes, the men went from house to house.

And we dragged them out, one by one. There stood the four of them, trembling like nesting hens.

"But we are not murderers," said the men, our men.

And they forced the four to dig a grave for Justino. Right there where they'd murdered him.

And to kneel and ask the dead man for forgiveness.

And to recite the Credo for him. Under the sun. Praying in the hot sun, while we surrounded them with our machetes at the ready.

"We are the civil authorities," they said.

"You are the assassin authorities," our men said.

And each of the four had to throw at least one shovelful of dirt to give satisfaction to the dead man. After the burial they were set free.

"From fear of God more than anything else and because we're not murderers." We pardoned them.

Justino was avenged and the account of his death was settled. Justino was my uncle, son of Mama Lupe.

We never imagined the grief we would suffer as a result of the incident with the civil authorities.

When the officers realized what had happened, truck-

loads of guardsmen and even a helicopter and an airplane were sent. The slaughter was brutal: there were many deaths, houses were burned, women raped, children beaten. Even the animals had to pay a price. They took care of the chickens and the pigs with gunshots. The oxen and the horses were done away with with knives. Some men were able to escape to the mountains with their women and children. Through mountains and along roads we wandered.

Five days later, we started reappearing in the region; we couldn't stand the hunger. And our little brothers and sisters, their bodies couldn't stand the bites of mosquitoes and other nocturnal insects. The houses in seven villages were searched. From Ilobasco to Chalate the government's repression extended.

Almost all the houses in the area where Justino's death had been avenged were destroyed.

None of this appeared in the newspapers. They never say anything in favor of the poor. No one could work in this situation.

That's how the taking of the Cathedral came about. A group of students and teachers came to invite us.

And since we were already organized, well, we went along: one hundred and twenty farmworkers, plus a group of teachers and students.

Maybe this way the newspapers would say something about our situation.

On the agreed-upon day, we all began arriving for Mass.

Around ten in the morning, when Mass was over, we pretended we were sightseers and we stayed seated on the benches. Until someone said soon after, "Close the doors."

Then the priest who had stayed arranging the holy vessels came and said to us, "What are you doing?" And that "it

*would be better if you left." We told him that we weren't
going to move from there; that we were going to remain for
some time and would he lend us the keys to the doors of the
passageways to the church.*

*And no sooner had the priest refused to lend us the keys
than we were ready with a file. We cut inside the bolts and
closed up the church immediately, leaving only the main
door open. Two students and three teachers served as watchmen, explaining to people who came for baptisms and con-
firmations that services were suspended today for such-and-
such a reason. And that if they wanted to come in to say
prayers, they would have to do it quickly unless they wanted
to join us in our protest against the brutalities in the villages
of Chalatenango.*

*The people would listen to us, would cross themselves
and would run away as fast as their feet could carry them.
By noon, we were all inside, except for the watchmen. They
had the main door half open and from there they were
delivering a speech through a microphone. They were addressing onlookers who were gathering in the street.*

*And we inside, ready to close up in case of an emergency,
because the Cathedral was surrounded by policemen and a
few squad cars. We began to get help from the people, especially from the women in the market, in the form of food,
clothes, aspirins and alcohol. And in the midst of all of this
they hung some banners with messages on the outside of the
Cathedral.*

*In about an hour, at one o'clock in the afternoon, a priest
dressed in purple arrived and tried to convince us to leave:
"Listen, this is the worst place you could have chosen. You
better leave; there's no need to risk your lives. We know
that you have good reason for being here but there's no need*

149

to add to what has already happened to you." That's what he says to us. "I'm in charge of this holy place."

"Monsignor," says one of the students (until then I'd never met a monsignor). "We have faith that you and all the other Christians will not allow anything to happen to us."

And the monsignor tells us, "Well, I warn you, stay if you want. The only thing I ask is respect for all the things here; they're sacred."

And one of us says, "Monsignor, you can rest assured, we're honest people and, as you can see, our protest is peaceful—no one here has even a machete."

And the monsignor says, "Yes, but I see that you're capable of anything. You already broke the locks on the doors to the passageways."

And we tell him, "Yes, Monsignor, but that's because the priest would not lend us the keys and we did it for security, to be able to shut the door."

The monsignor was furious, but he was trying not to show it; he kept pulling on his cassock—it looked as if he was going to rip it. "Look, Monsignor, the blame does not lie with us," a teacher told him.

And the monsignor says, "You are forgetting that this is the most sacred place of Catholicism in El Salvador."

I tell you, I wonder why I said it, because I'm not used to talking to a monsignor, not even to a sacristan. I tell him, "That's why we're here, Monsignor." Sometimes the mind lights up. "Yes, that's just why we're here," almost everyone chimes in.

Suddenly another priest appeared, better dressed. "Pretty clothes," I say to myself. Someone whispered, "It's the archbishop." "How did he get in?" And everyone saying as

he approached, "the archbishop." "Monsignor Romero,"
someone said.

Then we began to applaud. Because we had heard talk of
him, that he defends us. And as he wasn't expecting this out-
burst from us, he began to laugh. He told the monsignor
that it was all right, that he would permit us to stay and not
to worry about the sacred things that were in the church.
Perhaps he was frightened by so many people. Well, he told
us, "You, there are enough of you."

And one of the organizers says, "There are one hundred
and thirty of us, Señor Archbishop, one hundred and twenty
come from Chalatenango—they're farmworkers—and ten of
us are from here."

And he told us that he knew all about our problem, that
on that same day he was going to meet right away with
those on top to solve the problem as soon as possible.

Then they took the one who had spoken up, the one in
charge, around the church to show him hiding places that
we could use in the event of an emergency.

After that, they left. The organizer got us together to tell
us that in the event of a necessity he would lead us to the
place that the priests had shown him.

At three o'clock a combination of lunch and supper was
served. It was abundant, it was brought from a dining room
and from the market. The food came in plastic bags. I had
never eaten food so delicious. We ate everything so that
nothing would spoil. Food from another world.

After a while Monsignor Romero returned to select people
who would cook; he told us, only these two persons could
enter his sacred kitchen. And he explained: only his relatives
and his cook have entered his kitchen. "Thank you very

151

much, Monsignor," someone said. And since he had the eyes
of a deer, he selected the only two primary school teachers
in our group. Then the teachers said they would need a
helper. I was chosen. "All right, then," Monsignor said.
"You already know, be very careful." "It'll be fine, Father,"
I said, so carried away that I was acting as if everything
was up to me.

Then were chosen those in charge of clean-up and
security.

That day I was not aware of time. I thought only about
my father and my mother. About my grandfather Chepe.

And I thought also about my grandmother Lupe. And my
three siblings: a brother one and a half years old, a sister
seven years old and a brother ten years old.

I didn't think about my father so much; it's true, after all,
he has disappeared, which is like being dead, and a principle
of mine is not to think about the dead because it leads to
sadness and sadness deflates the spirit.

My father's name is Helio Hernández.

He was the mainstay of the family. Now I am.

We endured many hard times at home.

But I'd better not think about that because it's pointless.

The little stove used gas; you know the kind, those that
one must be careful to light because they can explode. Those
that go poof when you put a match near them. In order to
have enough for everyone to eat, we had to begin cooking
at six in the morning and we would finish at ten. Lunch was
between eleven and three. We used plastic plates, the kind
you throw away. But we didn't throw them away. We washed
them. We the cooks didn't have time even to scratch our
noses.

We remained in the Cathedral for eight days. During that time almost no one was able to bathe. Only the cooks, because in the kitchen there was a little bathroom where we would throw water on ourselves and soap up with the soap we used to wash the dishes.

From the first day, security measures were taken. At most, only two persons at a time were allowed to go to the bathroom. At night we slept in two groups: one was called A and the other B. With our shoes on because in an emergency one could not run without shoes.

We had our first test one night when we heard the shout "Group A, Group B." We woke up in a fright because it turns out that the watchman had seen a group of policemen running toward the main entrance. It was only a warning because the only thing they did was tear down the banners with the messages that had been hung in front of the Cathedral.

For the rest of the night no one slept, and the one in charge called attention to those who had taken off their shoes and to the sleepyheads who had failed to wake up at the shout "Group A, Group B." He told us that it was three in the morning. I, for example, was last to get up, after they were all in their groups. He scolded those who had slept on the benches in front of the doors. And he advised them of how dangerous it would have been had there been an outburst of machine-gun fire. From that day on, we slept on the floor or on benches but all together or in groups, and in a place protected by a wall. During the daytime, so that we wouldn't be bored, someone would give a talk about rights, or songs were taught. Two days later Monsignor Romero came back, and since he found us making ourselves

153

at home, and no one acting very pious, he told us, "Well, I see that no one remembers the sacred place you are in."

And as one voice we said, "But of course we do, Monsignor!" And he told us, "Well, let's see, how many of you have prayed?"

We all raised our hands. I almost burst out laughing because, it's true, no one had remembered that we were Catholic or believers, and much less to pray, because we were not there for that. With the problems we had.

And the monsignor, in a serious tone, told us, "You don't fool me; you raise your hands from habit, not because you prayed."

Then the one in charge told him, also in a serious tone, "Monsignor, even though you may not believe it, we are all believers and we follow the commendments of God. That's right. But if at a given moment they were to 'touch' us, we would be obliged to defend ourselves."

The monsignor thought it better to change the subject. "How do you like the food? Is the kitchen functioning properly? Do you sleep well?" And then, changing the subject again, he told us, "On the radio they say that what you are asking for has already been taken care of. If you want to leave you can do so without fear, because there are orders to respect your lives; no one will be persecuted if you leave here."

And the one in charge answered him, "Thank you very much, Monsignor, for the news you bring, but we're not going to move until we receive orders from our leaders, because you guarantee our lives here but not when we return to our homes in the country. Besides, the guardsmen are still in the villages, and as long as they remain there we're not going back."

The monsignor preferred to excuse himself and he told us that he would return at nine the next morning to say Mass for us.

By the fourth day, food was running low, barely a bread or a cracker per person. At meetings it was said, "Be careful, you three little fat ones, because no one is going to perish from hunger with you here."

And they would say, "Don't be so mean, friends. Would you be capable of eating us roasted?"

And I, kitchen helper that I was, would say, "Yes, you people better be careful!" We all enjoyed the silly things we'd say.

The one in charge told us, "Be patient. Since the food ran out they're already making arrangements to get more through the Red Cross."

And as the Red Cross didn't show up, the next day it was said that it was necessary to go to the store, but clever people were required because the danger was great, as much in going as in coming; they could be arrested. It was necessary to take a taxi to expedite the shopping and to minimize the possibility of arrest.

Two girls volunteered: one was about fourteen, and the other sixteen. They left by the back door, on the convent side. It was ten o'clock in the morning. By four in the afternoon, we were worried because they had not returned—we thought that maybe they had been captured. Or that they had gotten scared and ran away, deserting us. "No, those girls have guts; it's just that since the church is being watched so closely they haven't been able to sneak back in," said the one in charge.

That's how it was, because soon thereafter the watchmen at the door saw them pass in a taxi; they circled the church about four times and then disappeared. What was happening was that no one could approach the church on foot because of the police, who were ready for anyone who went near the church; but the girls had gone around several times to get to know the layout and they saw that they could get the food through on the side of the church that was still under construction; you see, on that side the authorities weren't very vigilant. The girls gave the bags of food to the bricklayers and told them to pass them to the other side, where they would be picked up by the people closed off in the church. "Send these bags through there for us, please?" they said to the workers.

Then, without the bags, the girls went around to the convent side and who knows how they managed to convince the policemen on the corner, because they were allowed to pass. The convent is behind the Cathedral on the same block. As there was a policeman at the door of the convent, the girls went over to talk to him, and when they saw that the door had been opened to allow some visitors to enter and see the priests, they were ready and all of a sudden sprang inside. They left the policeman standing with his mouth open. Their arrival was greeted with applause. And they told us what had happened on their shopping trip. They told us to get some rope to haul the food in through a little window that faced the side of the church under construction and that connects with the bedroom and kitchen of the monsignor. Two experts at climbing were summoned—those who can climb coconut trees; you see, the window was about forty feet from the ground. In about half an hour the food was in our possession. It was five o'clock in the afternoon.

Then we prepared a good meal—for lunch each of us had had only half a cracker.

On the following day we received sufficient food from the Red Cross, although it wasn't a gift but a delivery from the women of the market and our organization.

Everything was all right except discipline, because to be locked up is disturbing, especially for the farmworkers who are used to being in the open air. The only ones who didn't get bored were the watchmen, who were hoarse from shouting through the sound apparatuses, the microphones. Except for them, no one could see the street.

It was prohibited to look out the windows or doors; we looked only at the four walls. Maybe that's why every minute someone was asking permission to be excused, because that was the only way to walk around, because to get to the bathroom one had to go up and down stairs, through dark hallways until you reached another room, where masses were also held; two or three seminarians, and three or four relatives of the monsignor in charge of the Cathedral, who are all young students and employees, also slept there. They couldn't or didn't want to leave. As to that monsignor, we all concluded that he was running the same risk as we and that at bottom he had not behaved badly, especially considering that old people are more concerned about their hide, and he was suffering from diabetes; that's what he told the cooks. Besides, he felt trapped, he had not wanted to leave, and besides, as he was the head of the Cathedral, it was to our advantage to have him there with us. On one of those days he said to the teacher-cook, "Look, God will reward you, because there's no need for you to be locked up here and you are doing something for your neighbor."

And then he said, "This is the second time I've fallen captive to the farmworkers; but now I don't have enough strength to remain locked up so long in the church." That was when he spoke of his diabetes. And the teacher-cook told him not to feel trapped, because he was assisting in a just cause. He only laughed and continued his prayers, with a little string with little beads in his hand that is called a rosary.

There were amusing things, for example, the falls resulting from the darkness of the hallways, and because there were so many stairs to go up and down.

And for those who were distracted, things did not go well; there was always someone getting into trouble, always someone shoving and pushing.

Once, several companions didn't have any coffee to drink because there wasn't enough to go around; you see, the person in charge of carrying it almost broke his nose falling down the stairs. When we went to the site of his fall, we saw the coffee on the floor. It really wasn't that dark. What was happening was that the steps blended into the color of the bricks above and below, and if you didn't take special notice it seemed flat, so a distracted person would walk into it and fall down.

Only a few had stomach problems. At first because we ate sparingly. Then because everything was well cooked. And we were very clean.

We were neglectful only once, when we confused a chamber pot with a cooking pot from the kitchen, and upon pouring out water for coffee we noticed the smell and threw it out. After that, we didn't use any more pots because of the nasty doubts resulting from that other confusion.

One day three bags of frozen meat, fish and chicken were received. The persons who sent them to us by way of the bricklayers on the outside were caught. That day a telephone call was received in the convent. Around eight o'clock we were still cooking bean soup when the monsignor's cook took the call and they told her, "Tomorrow you'll be out of there!" Nothing else. The woman told us, "I've just heard a very mean voice telling me that tomorrow you'll be out of here, but I don't know whether for better or for worse. Be careful." We told her, "Thank you very much, and please bring down the beans because we're going to tell the others the news."

To get to where all the others were, there was a door that the cooks could use as often as they wanted, though for the sake of security, we didn't abuse the privilege. From outside, we would knock twice so that our watchmen could open and let us through. Around there there was a crack allowing one to see the street although we never looked for reasons of discipline, and because it was dangerous, we always went by as quickly as possible. This time we decided to look through the crack and we noticed that there was little vigilance; the radio patrol cars disappeared except one. The policemen could be counted on one hand.

When we arrived, we saw that almost all of our companions were standing around a little radio that could barely be heard. We went over to the one in charge and related to him what the monsignor's cook told us.

He said not to tell anyone so that they wouldn't be disillusioned if it was just a trick. And that he too had noticed the lack of surveillance by the police—that's why they had turned on the little radio for the nightly ten o'clock news.

Right there we heard that the next day, at noon, the Cathedral would be evacuated under the auspices of the Red Cross.

Since we believed that there was no more danger, when we returned to the kitchen we decided to go up to the flat roof and we saw a big fire, about a block of houses, over there in the distance. I felt happy not because of the fire, but because we were going to leave and who knows, maybe everything was solved at our homes, in our villages.

And that's the way it was. The next day Red Cross buses arrived. Since then, I've been sleeping in the hills. We don't see our father because he's disappeared ever since the guardsmen took him away. My mother is still there, the poor thing, suffering, as my brothers and sisters are still little. The ten-year-old already goes to work and helps the family economically. So do I.

The worry persists, even if one is sure that so many hardships cannot be eternal. We are doing what's necessary so that they won't be eternal. For a few days the persecutions in our town and region were suspended. But they will return. But each time they will find us more powerful in our response. What with the despair of our mothers, sisters and grandparents, what we farmworkers have done revives us.

Everything came out all right. Meanwhile, I'm returning to Ilobasco.

12 NOON

Cuu-cuu goes the *tortolita* in the *maculís tree*. The cinnamon-colored *tortolita*, with a white stripe on its wings. Cuuu-cuuu, each time prolonging the "uus" like the murmur of a child. The *tortolita* is the sad dove. The dove, solitary and gentle. It sings to say that it's already twelve and the chicken isn't cooked yet. Cuuu-cuuu and it flies with a rustle of its wings toward the *tamarindo* branch. "Now the sun is at its peak." That same *tortolita* Adolfina will be hearing as she approaches the bend. Hot dust getting into her sandals. And the little ones walking on tiptoe. Slack-jawed, throwing stones at star lizards.

Over there they'll come, on the road with the lizards, *tihuilotes* and *maculises*, and the *tortolitas* announcing lunch hour.

Over there they'll come, disturbing the birds that are already hungry, because birds also eat at twelve just like any Christian.

There wasn't time enough to knead dough; hot tortillas with salt are always good. "On your way back bring tortillas," I told her, maybe that's why she has taken so long, waiting for them to be made. I woke up lazy this morning. "Tell my neighbor to make me three big tortillas and three little ones for the children." "All right," she tells me.

And the solitaire bird also awakes, whistling and sounding like a jail bugle, among the leaves of the *chilamate*, eating ripe *chilamates*. Fuili-fuiiii, says the solitaire bird, hidden in the moist humid moss of the ravines, drinking water from the puddles like fish. Watching himself in reflections from the little puddles.

And the *tortolita* responds to the solitaire.

And the *chiltota*, face of *zunza*. Singing like little kittens on the high branches of the ceiba tree. And the black robin, singer of *rancheras*, courts his female counterpart, who quiets the bandit, throwing him little yellow kisses of *zunsapote*. Along that road of songs comes Adolfina, Benjamin, Ester and Moncho.

—At last, here's the kid.

—Hurry, go to the door, I'll cover you.

"They're looking for you," I shout to her before they can surprise her. "Hurry up," I tell the children who have remained behind.

Pijiriche leaps.

"There comes my granddaughter," I say. Talking to myself. Nothing more because there she is, opening the door suddenly. Shouting, "Hurry up." With a pack of tortillas on her head. Balancing tortillas on her head.

"Hurry up, girl! You wouldn't walk so slowly even if you were playing pilgrimage." "It's just that I've been fighting with Moncho along the way because he didn't want to walk.

He fell asleep over at his godmother's, while she was making the tortillas."

The official takes out his notebook.

Asking what's your name, both paternal and maternal last names, who is your father, what do you do for a living, where are you coming from, how did you get to the Kilometer, are you in the Federation of Christian Farmworkers, since when, how old are you, what have you come to do at your grandmother's place.

And Adolfina:

—You're Private Martínez, aren't you?

And he:

—Can you believe this inquisitive child?

And the other meddlesome agent:

—Didn't I tell you, chief, these people are getting more insubordinate, more insolent.

And Adolfina:

—My mother and grandmother have told me about you. You went with William to my old grandfather's house, to my father's father's place.

And he:

—Look, child, I've heard enough from you. Maybe you have confused me with someone else. Stop misbehaving because here we're the ones asking questions; next thing you know, you'll be pulling out a notebook and taking notes . . .

The meddlesome one:

—It's just that these people aren't interested in working things out. The easier you are with them, the more they want to get shitty on you. Even if we didn't want to get angry, this is the kind of thing that makes you lose patience.

And he:

—Stop tempting me because already I'm capable of zapping this child on her dirty face. Isn't it true that you don't even bathe? Isn't it true that you fuck Communists?

And I:

—Look, sir . . . Sergeant, up to now we've been respectful of authority. You come here and we answer your questions. Although we're humble, we know how to be polite. I would like you to respect us, to finish whatever it is you are doing without insults. You must take into account that if the child questions you, it's because she has suffered much—her father has been imprisoned, her mother almost lost an eye from a whack the authorities gave her, and then they go to the child's grandfather's house. Imagine what we've had to put up with.

I don't tell him about your uncle Justino.

The meddlesome one:

—They think just because they're women . . .

And Adolfina:

—You people don't put too fine a point on anything, look how you kicked my mother, and I know that you, Mr. Private, had something to do with that, I know it very well, and what's more, I know your mother, Doña Patricia. Don't try to tell me it's a lie. I am the daughter of Helio Hernández. Where is he?

And I, grabbing her by the hand, pressing her against me:

—Child, don't be impudent. Respect the gentlemen and answer their questions. You understand, Mr. Sergeant, she's just a child and still feeling her tragedy. We aren't made of stone, and sometimes we behave badly when we have misgivings . . .

The meddlesome one:

—You see, there still are some polite old whores in the world . . . even if it's hard to believe.

And I:

—You are the ones who must tell us the purpose of your visit, but since you've been here without talking, well, that's what creates problems, because she, as you know, is just a minor still in the care of her family, you can't behave this way for no good reason, be understanding, Mr. Sergeant . . .

And he:

—Look, Señora, these things happen because of the lack of respect you've been having for the authorities recently, as if your shit had risen into your head. Be reasonable and you'll soon see that you won't be any the less for it. Tell your granddaughter to cooperate with us for everyone's sake. We'll do our job and come off smelling like a rose.

And I:

—What I want is for you not to speak that kind of language in front of her. For me there is no problem, because I'm old and used to everything.

And Adolfina:

—Well, then, tell me what you want from me.

And it seems to me that their intentions aren't bad.

Even though one can never know with these people.

12:10 P. M.

—We want to talk to you alone.

It's a miracle they used the formal "you" because they are not polite, especially when they decide to be mysterious.

—Well, you see, we found a wounded man, and as you passed that road earlier, well, we thought you may have noticed.

And that's what they couldn't tell, that's the reason for all this mystery! I think.

And Adolfina: —I haven't seen anyone.

—You passed that place at nine o'clock.

—Which place?

—Where we found the wounded man. They told us that you were on that road. And then the wounded man mentioned a name that sounded like Adolfina.

—Well, look, I don't know what you're talking about . . .

—That wounded person will not tell us his name and it turns out that he doesn't even have identification papers, and we said, well, let's go look for the Adolfina mentioned by this wounded man, and as you are the only one by that name around here . . .

—But you say you're not very sure?

—There you are, very sure we're not. Otherwise we wouldn't be asking you. Everything would have been cleared up at once.

—And you, what do you want?

—To see if you will go with us, if you recognize him, in case you know him, help us a little.

—Wouldn't it be better to take him to the hospital, if he is as seriously wounded as you say?

—Look, you don't have to tell us anything; we came to get you. Leave those tortillas that you're carrying and let's go.

And I tell them no, what for, since if that wounded man knows Adolfina he must know me too; it would be better if I went with them and she remained with the children. In fact, better if we all went. And they: "Don't get involved, old whore, we don't have time for this and the man is several miles away and how are you going to haul these kids to such a serious legal affair." And I, knowing them, say Adolfina is not leaving this house, is not going to take even one step alone. "You will understand that she is a child and that she has been entrusted to me, she's my granddaughter. I can't let anything happen to her while she's in my care. Take me. I can walk long distances as well as you and let's see about leaving the children with my neighbor. I could recognize the man if he is from around here. I know everyone, unless he's from some other place, in which case he isn't our problem and there's probably been some mistake, you yourselves admit that possibility; you must understand my reasons, I'm in mourning, as you can see, not long ago a loved one of mine died, and that's why I'm nervous and I won't let the child leave. I'd rather that you shot me right here, if that's what makes you happy, but my granddaughter will not budge from here, you will have to kill us all."

I didn't even know what I was saying. I could only hear the voice of Adolfina, "Wait grandmother maybe we can all go together with no problem. Don't get that way, we're all going. Isn't that right gentlemen of authority, isn't that right gentlemen of authority that all of us can go?" Meanwhile I was telling myself what had happened before, gathering strength, because I wasn't going to allow her to be taken from me just like that, after what happened to Justino, by men who didn't seem well intentioned to me at that moment. They, not budging an inch, only giving orders, looking at me strangely—maybe after so many hours of silence I surprised them by all of a sudden talking so much; the truth is, they were only watching me, thinking perhaps this old woman is crazy, what's the matter with her. That's how these old whores are. Nothing mattered to me; I wasn't even thinking about my little children, nor whether they would put a bullet through me. The children were crying streams of tears, with the noise of children when they cry when they're hungry, when they're hurting, when they're sick. "My granddaughter is not going anywhere," I shouted until even Pijiriche began barking at me. Adolfina hugging me, still without putting down the pack of hot tortillas. "Don't be like this," Grandmother, she on the verge of tears. "Don't be like this." Crying. Justino would condemn me if I were to let her go with those men. And thinking of him, I gathered more strength. They will have to kill me first; they will have to kill all of us.

Until they finally spoke:

—This old woman is going to have a fainting fit.

—What an hysterical old woman.

—Either you let the child go or we'll take her by force, against your will. This old woman sure fucked up everything. This is what we get for being nice guys.

Then Adolfina spoke:

—I will not go with you, I'm not moving from here, I don't know who it is you want me to see. You'd better take us all, even if it takes us a while to get there. If it's not too far, the children can walk and we'll carry the little one. I don't see any problem.

Wiping her eyes with the apron that she had put on early in the morning. The poor thing, speaking to them so naturally that they wouldn't even have noticed she was crying had she not wiped her face and her eyes, which were like sparkling marbles full of tears.

—These people keep getting more and more abusive, I wonder where they get the nerve . . .

—It would be better if *they* were the authorities, because one can't give orders around here anymore.

—I've never seen a more stubborn pair of bitches.

—The only thing they understand is a good beating. If you want, we'll get tough, as we should, and stop fucking around.

—Wait, you, I'm the one who gives the orders here, don't get carried away.

And then all of a sudden Adolfina repeats what she had said before, she with her ideas, and she tells him: "Look, I know you. I've been wondering where I'd seen your face before; you're the son of Ticha, the lady who sells vegetables in the market on Sundays."

"These people sure know how to get your goat; it's as if they were discussing matters!" And then he tells Adolfina: "Look, I don't even know you, I don't even know who Ticha is! Stop being disrespectful toward the authorities and let's go."

—You came to my mother's house.

—That bitch is crazy, sir. She's provoking us for the hell of it; they don't want things to go well.

"Stop it, child, the past is not important; don't show a lack of respect." "It's not something that's over and done with, Grandmother," she tells me in a low voice, there where I'm holding her against my chest.

And the man took out a little radio, pulled out what they call an antenna and began talking with numbers, asking by telephone if it were possible to bring the wounded man. Speaking into the strange gadget, that the jeep should come this way, with the man.

The little children, huddled in the corner of the cart, were playing with the head of Pijiriche, were eating their tortillas with beans. "Children, go play in the yard, get out of the corn or you'll be covered with *ajuate* pollen." And they go with the dog trailing them. And I caught myself watching them, as if I were saying goodbye, because that's how it is in these times—every minute you must say goodbye to loved ones in case you never see them again. One never knows the final occasion, the last time you'll see them with their eyes open, alive—well, the dead remain with their eyes open, like Justino. His eyes looked as if they were made of glass, his head stuck onto a post. And something of a smile on his lips or maybe he was saying goodbye to his children, or to me, or to his companions for whom he was looking out.

So, every time you leave me for a while, Benjamin, tall and strapping. Ester, you're so skinny the wind will carry you away. Moncho, little nursling. And Adolfina, blood of María Pía and of my blood. I always signal goodbye, just in case. And I also entrust myself to God.

That's how things are now. One never knows where the blow will come from.

And when I think about God, I also think about the conscience that Chepe talks about. Maybe they're the same thing. What would become of me without a conscience? I wouldn't be able to withstand these things. How will those people without a conscience endure the pain? Those who don't have Chepe? My heart goes out to them. Horrible.

They continue talking into the little radio, pressing buttons and talking.

Go leave those tortillas inside; pretty soon we'll be able to eat our little rice in peace. Leave them wrapped tight so they won't get cold. I don't know how men become accustomed to eating cold tortillas, because at work what they get is practically shoe leather instead of tortillas, the famous *chengas*, heavy and rancid. Tortillas, either they're eaten hot or they're not tortillas.

It's nice to be aware. One suffers less.

Suddenly, the afternoon lights are aflame. I see the breasts of the *tortolitas* making as if they were the bellows of the blacksmith. Their cinnamon-colored feathers. Their heads to one side, the better to listen to the cuu-cuu of other *tortolitas* farther away, calling to each other from great distances, without needing little radios, or antennas. Every afternoon they come to eat corn crumbs. During the season of *tortolitas*, they boldly appear and descend even

171

down to the cart. Then they go to the *tamarindo* tree. To eat the little bits of corn they've collected. The sound of their wings flapping, when they're frightened. Rum-m-m. Fluttering rumm-rumm.

"If you want, eat while I keep the guardsmen company, get your rice and a couple of spoonfuls of beans and give it to the children for me, one spoonful for each. You brought salt, didn't you, my dear?" A little fistful for each. Salt is cheap but it shouldn't be wasted. It's a sin. They baptize one with salt to erase original sin. I baptize you in the name of the Son and of the Holy Spirit. It seems that only yesterday we took Adolfina to have water sprinkled on her. She has grown a lot lately; soon she'll get married on us. And have children.

Well, one day Chepe says to me: "If I'm called on to shed blood, my blood, it doesn't matter because it is for the good of everyone else." That's the way he is. "Conscience," he tells me, "is to sacrifice oneself for those who are exploited." I would never have known the meaning of that word if Chepe hadn't explained it to me. It was hard for me to take that word in, to understand why we're exploited. Because for me everything was part of nature. He who is, is. Everyone carries his own destiny. I used to believe in those things. If one is poor, well, that's life. What are we going to do if God didn't reward us with a better life. We should thank him for keeping us healthy and for giving us sufficient corn, salt and beans. Until we began to discover the meaning of the word "exploited." We farmworkers are exploited in this country. Our poverty arises from this. If they were to pay us well, that would be another matter. But we would always be exploited. The children must go to school so that they won't grow up ignorant, he tells me, so that they'll better understand the problem of ours, of the farmworkers!

Chepe is always thinking of others. And he acts on it, and because of that spirit of solidarity he's loved by everyone. They know that he is always ready to sacrifice himself for others. The change in him came after he joined the organization of ours; he even quit drinking in order to dedicate himself fully to its activities. Saturdays and Sundays don't exist for him. At first, I didn't understand why he used to leave us abandoned; it wasn't that he'd go away, but that he wouldn't give us any attention—only the work of the organization existed for him. He would explain his reasons to us. "This way of being, it is having conscience," he tells me. And, you see, it is a complicated thing, it can't be defined by a single word. Conscience is all the things we do for the benefit of others without seeking our own interest.

And I say: Chepe is my conscience.

1 P.M.

And we eat a little food. Minutes are passing while they leave us alone because they're busy with the radio. At that moment, the chicken hawk appears gliding, swimming in the wind. Swift arrow, sharp-eared, the chicken hawk. Cuerk-cuerk, in the yard across the way. Like an avalanche descending on the flock of chicks. Like the wind he descends upon the trees of ripe mangoes, knocking down fruit in one fell swoop. That's how the hawk descends upon the chicks. The hen fights the hawk; she throws herself on top of him, but the hawk takes flight and the hen can barely leap a few inches in the air. And she runs toward the others, as soon as she has lost one of her children: cluck-cluck.
—That's what I'm saying: when bad luck comes we're ruined, Don Sebas. Before, it didn't used to rain, and when the rain came like cat piss, we were so happy because we could sow our little corn. All that we suffered last year.

174

—Maybe this will be a good year; for several days now
many ducks have been passing by.

—You don't say, really, Don Sebas? I haven't even seen
them, with the joy one feels watching them fly so
high.

Maybe because the rain is going to be strong, you can't
imagine the number of ducks flying in a V for victory in
the sky.

—They're going to the North Pole, perhaps?

—I wonder where in hell they're going.

—One must have faith this year.

"It's already raining by the volcano, wetting my Papa
Juan", I like to sing each time I see over there on the
horizon the rain walking from afar, getting closer and closer,
taking its time to arrive. "It still has a long way to go."
There's time to run to the Detour to buy molasses for coffee
at Don Sebas's place. And to get back with the rain on
one's heels. Just in time. Because we're so elevated, we see
it coming, a curtain on the horizon. And I sing: "It's already raining by the volcano." There's a great happiness.

—Ay, Mama, you know, after tasting the coffee you make,
when I try someone else's, I notice the big difference. You
better tell me your secret so I can pass it along to my
friends . . .

—You're just saying that because it's made by your Mama.
Well, it's the best . . .

—Really, Mother . . .

—You'll see when you get married and leave this home,
then the most delicious coffee will be the one your wife
makes. That's life, Justino, part of the love people share.
The thing by itself isn't enough; it depends on how it's

given, the tenderness involved in giving it, the love in
receiving it . . .

—Well, you know, it's just that I'm almost twenty-one and
I'm still not married . . .

—I'm sure that here and there you must be flirting with a
girl; it's normal, son.

—Since I've thrown my body and soul into the federation,
we barely have time for that kind of foolishness.

—Those things are part of life, too, son.

It always seemed to me that he was the living image of
José, the same eyes and the same mouth; precisely like him,
while he wipes sweat from his brow, because he's just arriving, and then he lowers his hand so smoothly. Maybe
because it's the same gesture, I see you as if you were him,
José as a very young man, when he had just started coming
to the house. You dress better than José, Justino, because
he always wore a coarse shirt—he didn't own anything else—
whereas you, you have never liked rough material since
you lost your innocence, and you would go to town and always take great care in picking the shirt you were going to
buy. Always. Because young people nowadays are different;
they enjoy better things, although now men are in greater
danger. Since we are no longer silent and we demand our
rights, life has become impossible for men in these parts. We
were born poor and they would like for us to continue being
poor or finish us off. We see that by the way they treat us,
by the way they get rid of people so easily. We live in
poverty. We live with hunger and still they would like to
exterminate us; they don't want us to exist, maybe. Well,
who is going to pick the cotton? Who is going to pick the
coffee beans? Who is going to clear the fields so they can

sow with ease? Who is going to work those big plantations they own? Maybe they're going to do it? Maybe the authorities are going to exchange those automatic beasts they carry to intimidate people for a machete and a pair of oxen? Well? Are they going to take off their uniforms, too? Are they going to stop being the authorities who tramp all about, spying? Is all this going to happen when they finish off the poor?

"None of this will occur," Justino used to tell me. And José repeats to me, "But we have to organize ourselves." And for that reason we become strong and cease to be afraid. And if we are frightened, frightened of being left alone, we go on just the same. We won't let their cruelties, craziness and killings bother us. To be upset all the time would be like death itself. How can we ever give up when we're right?

—I don't know why I've been remembering Justino . . .

—We have to forget him.

—Don't tell me that you've succeeded in keeping him out of your mind. For several nights running I've heard you making little noises through your nose, sniveling as if you were ashamed, and then you had better go take a piss, that's what you say, and you take forever out there. I hear you urinating. You really are pissing, but you remain out there, as if haunted by memory.

—I haven't forgotten him, but neither do I want you to remind me of him, because it saps one's strength, this business of remembering children who we will never see again. We must keep ourselves calm so as to dedicate alertness of mind to our federation.

And he got up calmly today. He tells me, "Have the

children pick up all those corncobs thrown on the ground and put them in an old sack. My neighbor has been asking me for them for the fire."

As he was leaving at dawn this morning, he told me, "Maybe I'll return before sunset; sleeping in the hills is beginning to tire me out, even though I get along well with my companions."

"No, you'd better not come," I tell him. As long as there is danger; look what happened to Helio. They won't give the poor man up, they won't even say a word about him; at least we could see Justino's body, we know he is dead. It's worse, the anguish for a disappeared person; at least consolation comes with death. With a disappeared person they kill two birds with one stone: all of the living who revolve around the disappeared are chained to anguish. And anguish is a slow form of death.

And he is surprised that I know about Helio. "Who told you, how do you know?" At first he thinks it's Adolfina. "It wasn't her," I tell him. "Excuse me, but I didn't want to tell you so as not to worry you," he says. "It has been our year of bad luck," I say. "Bad luck does not exist; each person creates his own life, which is made of realities," he tells me. "How I found out doesn't matter; what's important is that we all should share this price of truth that is our lot. I will always be with you in any circumstance," that's what I tell him. And I am immediately sorry because he suddenly gets sad. "Don't worry," he tells me, as he prepares to go.

Because of the danger he leaves very early, when it's still dark and not a soul is on the roads. I watch him walking into the distance. "Imagine, today the hawk was around here, in the yard across the way."

* * *

And he will say to me, "Well, then, be careful with yours, because the hawk that eats chicken comes back for more." That's the way it is.

And I'm going to tell him, "As if he'd chosen it, he took off the fattest chick; the poor hen wanted to fly after him and then began to cluck, protecting the other chicks with her wings. It was so sad." Must there be hawks?

And he will say to me, "The loss of any child hurts. Even animals miss their dead young." They say that even trees feel it when one cuts off a branch.

He told me, "Fortunately, the girl is going to stay a few days, to help you with little things. It's better that she be here because of how dangerous it is in Ilobasco; they say the authorities are having one of their stupid field days."

I tell him, "Look what they've done to María Pía, keeping her so in the dark, not telling her anything about Helio."

He tells me, "And the worst thing is when they stop saying anything about someone, and one never knows his whereabouts."

I'm surprised by Adolfina's strength. I don't know if the new generation is stronger. Her mother sent word that she will stay with us for about two weeks.

And I'm going to tell José, "You should see how helpful Adolfina is to me; I feel rested when she comes." Because she helps me with the children, her uncles and aunt. That makes her laugh. It's because I gave birth to Moncho when I was forty. Around that age more or less. The little baby is lucky for being spoiled by everyone in the family. "Poor child," he says, referring to María Pía. "To think she gave birth to such a strong and brave offspring as Adolfina."

We were talking about these things when the rooster flew down from the *tamarindo* tree. The loud noise he makes with

his wings as if he were pulling stars down from the heavens.
The rooster crows. Asking how many times Christ was denied. Christ already knew he would be denied.

We all suffer in one way or another.

Worse than being crucified. Or the same.

1:30 P. M.

I shit from laughter.

He makes me mess on myself every time he tells the
story. It happened because he was naughty. He doesn't
deny it, on the contrary. When he's in a good mood, he'll
retell it and retell it. To his grandchildren, to his young
children. To me. "Well, look at what happened with me and
that woman." And he recounts the same story.

He doesn't stop talking.

Well, I was in search of *altamiza* for María Pía's stomachache; she was nine months old then. I got to my mama's to see
if I can borrow Cañafistola. "And what's the matter, son?"
"My daughter has gotten sick on me and I'm going to the
river to look for *altamiza.*" "Oh, but darkness will fall on
you." My parents told me, "Go on, take her. Over there is
the blanket and saddle." And I left on Cañafistola. It was
barely five o'clock in the afternoon.

But at that time of the year by five o'clock it was already dark. I was almost grown up, nearly eighteen years old. I'd gotten off work at four and gone straight home. There was danger, the slaughter of '32 had just occurred. But I went to the river. What a fool! Can you believe it, riding around in the dark. The sun was already sinking into the coffee bushes behind the fog of those hours that send shivers up my spine. Anyone is in danger in the dark on a solitary road like that of the river. Thinking as much, I saw a figure sitting on a rock and the figure was not bad. The closer I got to it, the more I could tell that it wasn't bad, the figure, because it was a beautiful woman with long hair. She was colorful, but very dirty. I wondered who had left her there, abandoned. When I approached her to see if I could help, I noticed she was wearing nothing underneath her dress. I could tell by the trembling of her breasts. I noticed the cloth of her dress trembling with each palpitation of her heart, as if it contained quicksand or like a pond when struck directly by moonlight, the water won't stay still as it ripples.

And emotion clouded my eyes.

Her hips, a clay pot filled with fresh water. Her dimples were deep enough to hold marbles. Her eyes shone brightly, like velvet or the eyes of a snake. Her eyes looked straight ahead; her hips and the dimples, she wouldn't stop smiling.

Imagine, it didn't occur to me that she could be the dirty one.

And I say to her: "Why are you sitting on that rock? Don't you feel the heat? You could get the pissing sickness."

And she tells me: "Well, no, this rock is nice and cool, just right for sitting on, but the only thing is that I've been abandoned here."

I tell her: "Well, now you won't be alone any longer, if I could be at your service in any way you'd like."

Sincerely I tell you I had jumped off the deep end.

"Don't worry," she tells me—she wouldn't get the pissing sickness; well watch out. And I wasn't going to get flustered; you see, I was youthful and hot in the pants. "I said what I said for your own good." Just remembering the whole thing makes my hair stand on end. And I continued to make the acquaintance of the stranger without noticing the shadows that slowly envelop us. She filled the silence of the coffee field. And I ask her: "What are you doing out here, all alone?" She tells me that she is not alone. I looked around and there is no one else. I look like a fool, I don't see anyone. "You are with me," she says. My heart starts to beat again. Well, then, we're alone in this solitude. "That's the way it is," she says. And I, like a dog, wanting to jump all over her. And I ask her to accompany me, "I'm going to the river to get some *altamiza*, and then I'll take you to wherever you wish." Throughout my voice was trembling and my heart was leaping like a cat within me. Pum-pum, it went from emotion, almost paralyzing me. Her waist, the neck of a jar. "Get on, then." I help her climb on and put her in front of me, so she wouldn't fall off and hurt herself. Squeezing her; don't worry, I ride holding her tight, so she wouldn't be hurt by the jolts of the beast. And all he did was bounce up and down, just for the fun of it, I'm sure, taking advantage of the situation.

"I'll go with you later, I tell you," she whispers.

Don't worry, I told her, just show me the way and I'll take you there, and the worst part of it is that I lied so as not to make her jealous. One can be so foolish. "The *altamiza* is for a little old lady, a neighbor of mine in the village, who suddenly got a stomachache." Surely I was a candidate for this woman, perhaps because of my youth and my horniness. And worse, all the time she was telling me about the flowers along the road and the fish in the river.

I say to her: "Do you like *pepescas*?"

She says: "No, I don't."

"Then why did you say you like the *olominas* from the river, they are the same thing?" I asked.

"Because it's not the same thing," she responded.

"It's the same thing," I tell her. "*Pepescas*, they are dried *olominas* that are eaten fried, and *olominas* are *pepescas* when they are alive," I finish explaining.

"Well, that's how it is," she clarifies. "I like little fish, nice and fresh and alive, I don't like dried little fish, dead little fish."

And I made the first move. As one can be dense, one doesn't understand at first, still I tell her: "You're such a joker." We proceed: she's nice and snug against me, like a couple of frogs. All because of my badness. It was as if I'd won the lottery.

He's told me the story more than ten times; he always remembers it when he's happy. The first time he told it to me, I was a little jealous, but only at the beginning.

In reality, it was different. My mother-in-law tells me that he arrived home nearly frozen, he believed he'd seen the devil. He would not release the *altamiza*, he carried it pressed to his chest. Deaf and dumb, frozen and pale. It was impossible to get him to say a word. Was he bitten by a snake or had the devil come after him? Nothing. He wouldn't let go of the *altamiza*. It was funny. My mother-in-law enjoys telling the story, too.

He continues recounting:

And I imagined her lying on the rocks naked; it was only a matter of taking off her dress and there you have it. I had already noticed while squeezing her, while I put my hands around her navel, carelessly raising them to touch her breasts, in step with Cañafistola. I tell her that she has the most beautiful hair around these parts. She tells me not to be such a liar, you know I'm ugly. Because she was a beautiful whore, or so I thought when I put her on the horse. I ask her if those breasts had an owner. She tells me it depends. And I get even crazier. Already I feel like I'm mounting her. The moment I saw her I fell in love with those dimples. I tell her. And with her eyes, brilliant as fireflies. And the whore says to me, "Imagine how much brighter they would be if you were to look directly into them."

"How are your eyes when one looks directly into them," I ask her. "It's better that you see them when we reach the river," she says. "Ah, little fool, don't be ridiculous, what could it matter?" I say.

Then as a complaint she says: "You're holding me so tight I can't even move, I can't turn around. How can I show you my eyes if I can't turn around? Don't be impatient, and anyway, raise your hand a bit" I was out of control; I didn't know what to do with my hands, which were behaving like *masacuata* snakes, wanting to eat her with my fingernails, with my fingers. And I tell her: "It's just that you drive me crazy!"

She tells me: "You're nothing but a big seducer, you're even picking at the hair on my skin."

And I began to feel ashamed. I relax my hold on her a little. Imagine my surprise when she said: "I didn't mean like that." What more could I have asked for, imagine!

To get my way I tell her: "Why is it that it seems to get colder as we descend to the river?" I was really feeling it. "It's the cold air of the bald one." That's what she tells me. "You say I'm a womanizer, well, you're a tease." I tell her the truth. "You make fun of people," I say, acting the saint. "Well, you should see how much warmer I feel as we get closer to the river." When she mentions the river, the great heat of maleness circulates throughout me, and I can't stand it. Darkness comes and goes. So that it won't come, I double and cross my fingers; the pleasure was in contemplating her, admiring her body shaped like an earthen jar. The sun was trapped by the tallest *guarumo* trees. The truth is, the road belongs to Cañafistola; he directs, even getting his feet tangled up, tangling his feet, as if he had divined and contracted my fevers. Her breasts, for what reason would I lie, like two little doves with hard little beaks.

Even Cañafistola picked up his canter. "What could be the matter with this beast." The whinnying of the horse scattered the birds dozing in the branches. I feel the runnn-runnn of their frightened wings. The owls hoot. "He must have seen snakes, probably *tamagas*," I say. He refuses to go any further. I kick him with my spurs, he won't budge. "Hurry up, creature of burden, can't you see we've almost reached the river."

Everything that goes up must come down: maybe we should get down here, when all is said and done a nice, smooth rock formation that I was eyeing would be as good as the stones of a river. "Let's look for the *altamiza* around here," I tell her, and then I would take her wherever she wished. Because one is a dog with women. "Let's get down, then." And she, coquettish: "Ah, no, may you want to do something to me." "Don't be ridiculous," I say. "Can't you see that the beast refuses to budge; nothing bad is going to happen to you." Then the whore tells me: "What I want is for something good to happen to me."

Why did she have to tell me that: my legs began to tremble.

And then: "I'm going to tell you the truth. I had counted on a little darkness by the river, because there the elevation is low and night comes quickly, but here I'm afraid."

"Afraid of what?" I ask her.

She tells me: "Afraid of the light." "Well, you must be very shy," I tell her. And thinking that she was hinting at something: "Come on, let's go over to the cliffs, down there there's *altamiza*," thinking that down there it was darker and that she wouldn't deny me in a dark nook. She refuses to walk. "Move, don't be foolish, let's go to the cliff." Her head bowed, her hair falling over her face. I grabbed her a little roughly, tugging her. As they say: "Come with daddy." "Don't pull me, I'll come if I feel like it," she tells me. And then, while I put my hand there where she keeps her two turtledoves, she speaks to me in a different voice, almost like another person: "You see, I am the daughter of darkness." "Above the cliff there is light, but a little below it's already night, let's go and you'll see." I wasn't born yesterday. And with her two little doves in my hands, I wanted to suck their sweet milk. Then I noticed a light shining through her hair, like light from the eyes of a cat. I, believing in my imagination or in the beauty of her eyes, ask her: "Why do your eyes shine so much?" "You should see how they look in the dark," she tells me.

Well, when the urge comes over us, who can stop us? You can't deny she was giving me the opportunity and we men can't waste it or they'll speak ill of us. They'll even put you down as a faggot.

"Well, let's go where it's dark to admire them," I tell her, each time making an even bigger fool of myself. And as she walks calmly toward the cliff, she says: "That's nothing, look at my little fingernails." I suddenly saw the longest fingernails I had ever seen; they must have grown instantly or maybe because of emotion, I hadn't noticed, and I don't recall having touched her hands . . . well, one tends to be more direct in these cases of a woman alone found by a man on a secluded road. And even more if she is a coquette. If the man is a womanizer, for example. Although I've never been a womanizer; but temptation is temptation. And then she tilted her head back, uncovering her face which had been covered by her hair: there were no beautiful dimples, she was as pale as death. Immediately I let her go because I felt her suddenly become icy cold. At last she says: "And that's nothing, look at my teeth."

I suddenly saw the biggest teeth I'd ever seen in my life. No sooner had I heard her laugh than I shit in my pants right there. She ripped open her blouse and screamed at me: "Here are your tits, here are your tits!" I don't know how I didn't turn into stone or how I reached Cañafistola.

By the *guarumo* trees, her voice had faded: "Here are your tits, here are your tits." When I arrived home I was burning with fever. I don't even know how I got there.

And my grandmother says to me: "Why do you look like the face of death?" And for the life of me, I could not find the words. I had lost the power of speech. And what's more: "Since you've shit on yourself, what happened to you?"

I stayed in bed for more than five days. They say I would not let go of a sprig of *altamiza*, held against my chest. I wonder when I picked it.

So, whenever any woman would smile at me, I would see the *Siguanaba*.

You should see how José recounts this encounter with the *Siguanaba*. Hear it directly from him. Well, now he no longer even remembers it.

"Just think," José tells me, "that for more than ten days I drank only a corn concoction and ate white cheese, as if I had been a little child. I couldn't keep anything else down." Someone had said: "Give him children's food; it's mushier." "And everyone came to see if I would tell the story. It was more than a month before I could."

My mother-in-law says: "The first time he told it to me, it was as if he were confiding a secret, because it pained him to recount his roguery with the *Siguanaba*. 'If I don't tell you, I'm not going to pay for my sin,' he said to me. 'It's my only cure.' That's how it started. Once he had told me, he began to feel better. I told him I forgave him."

Since that was the story of his life, he told it for several years and each time embellished it a little. The final versions make us piss from laughter.

José now thinks it was all a dream.

2 P. M.

Right then we saw a cloud of dust over the fences. "Here comes the jeep with the man," Private Martínez says; well, that's what Adolfina told me his name was. And it stopped in front. Four guardsmen got out dragging the man, pulling him as if he were a sick animal. He was so disfigured, you couldn't even see what he looked like because of all the blood covering his face and drenching his shirt and pants. —Bring him over here to see if they know him.

It wasn't until I got close that I realized it was you, that you had your face covered with blood, and I could see that one of your eyes was tattered, one eye that had observed the life around here, because the eye was showing, it was hanging out. And then they asked Adolfina: "Do you know him?" "How am I going to know him if you bring him bathed in blood. I don't even know who it could be. You can't even see his face, I don't understand how you could think that anyone would recognize this man." That's what

Adolfina told them; she shouted instead of speaking, always addressing the one she called Private Martínez. And that's when I started sensing that I knew you, but I had my doubts. I don't know you and I don't want to know you. When I see your pants, my head is filled with nightmares. I don't know you, I don't know you. From where do I get the idea that I don't know you? Who instructed me to deny knowing you, or was my hope that it really wasn't you? Who could have had that exact pair of pants, a similar shirt, even though with all the blood it was barely distinguishable, did you ever have a shirt the color of blood? And why were they looking for Adolfina and not for me who could have identified you? What was the motive? Why that torture, that evil in the hearts of men who also had a mother, a father, children, sisters? Who had perverted them and watered down their blood? Theirs was not blood of the race, nor of Christians, nor of poor people, the blood that ran through their veins. What rabid bitch had adopted them as sons and had turned their blood into orgeat instead of the common fluid blood of human beings?

Adolfina's voice interrupts and tells me, "Grandma, what is happening to you?" And the voice of the authorities saying, "Perhaps you know him?" My legs on the point of giving out, my blood on the point of giving up, of ceasing to flow through my veins. I felt paleness scurrying all over my skin. "Do you know this man?"

My body turns to ice as I see you transformed into a piece of meat bitten by dogs, because I could see your body through the rips in your clothes, looking as if they had grabbed you and growled at you, pulling off chunks of flesh, sucking your blood. These vampires, sons of a hundred thousand whores, killers of the dirtiest stripe.

191

Then I said no. It had to be a no without any quavering of my voice, without the least trace of hesitation. And at that moment your good eye opened, the one they had left you, which perhaps for that reason you had kept closed so as not to talk, so as not to be recognized. Your coffee-colored eyes, the same ones I had seen with my pair for more than thirty years.

You are you, José, because that eye doesn't look like any other. You are you, I am sure of that, even if you hide from me. And God illuminated my mind, maybe, because I remembered your saying to me, "If at any time you detect danger to yourself or to our family, don't hesitate about denying me." And you made me swear. I never believed it would come to that. "Because, as for us, we're always in danger. Remember Justino, remember Helio, and all the others, we cannot afford to sacrifice blood needlessly," that's what you told me. "Leave it to me to save myself, if you see that there's no other way," you always repeated.

I saw that there was no other way out. And that's why you opened your eye when I had denied you, because I had already done the most difficult thing. I took it as a greeting, as if you were saying, "Thank you, Lupe," with that glance from your coffee-colored eye that had remained shut, shut by the same blood that bathed your head; while your other eye had been put out forever, hanging over your nose. I wondered how you managed to stay conscious. And the two men were holding you by your clothes from behind, as if you were a scarecrow.

I have not failed you, José. I understand that you were saying goodbye when you opened your eye, and besides greeting me, that you were proud of me, seeing me standing, with my arm around the shoulders of your granddaughter. And I remembered. I am remembering what you told me: "When I die, leave me with my eyes open, because I want to see it all, where one takes one's first steps in the other life. Only put my hands across my heart so as to think that I am taking you with me, holding you tightly to my chest." Throughout all of our life you've told me something like that.

"Well, I don't think I'm going to die calmly lying on a bed made of sticks," you have often told me.

I know that you are standing only because they're holding you up. You wouldn't have wanted to come back here and yet you still had the strength to say goodbye. As they say: "Behave yourself, don't faint, stay with me because I had promised to sacrifice my blood for a just cause." In those moments you were keeping your word and I was keeping mine. I promise you, I will keep mine.

"It's nothing, my child," I tell her.

"It's just that you seemed as if you were about to faint," she tells me.

"It is the reaction one would have in front of anyone, my child," I tell her.

Private Martínez: "Do you know him or don't you?"

I: "No, I don't know who he could be."

He brought him only so you would see how all bandits affiliated with the whatchamacallit peasant federation end up, that's what will happen to all of you. So says a cavernous voice from the other world.

Private Martínez: "We know that your granddaughter is going around getting mixed up in foolishness. You just saw how she misbehaved with me a while ago."

I: "I don't know what my granddaughter has been up to. I only know that she is a child who has other ambitions because we old people are half dead; we have allowed you to kill us slowly. But we've come to our senses while it's not too late. My granddaughter is alive and you are not going to kill her slowly. I know it, and it is what you don't like. She lives for all of us, she breathes for us, she is being born while we are in our death throes; it is also possible that she will save us."

I don't know how I uttered these words. I had to close my eyes. I have to close my eyes to be able to speak. So as not to see you, José, so your inspiration can reach me better.

Private Martínez: "We want you to look in this mirror. That's how you're going to end up, all of you who don't love the rich, because the enemies of democracy have poisoned your hearts, the hearts of all of you so you'll hate the rich people."

Adolfina: "If you don't have anything else to do, if you have enjoyed giving all of this abuse, you may go eat the gentleman you have hanging there."

The buck private: "Sir, don't let them be so disrespectful. If you want, I'll take care of this bitch."

Private Martínez: "Don't butt into what's none of your business. The girl is right."

Because you know the truth, Private Martínez, you know; you do it to torture us, to take out on Adolfina what you haven't been able to do with Helio, because otherwise he wouldn't have disappeared, because when people don't talk, nor are intimidated by your tortures, what you do is make them disappear. I don't know you, Private Martínez, but José enabled me to know all of you as a group. From where you are coming to where you are going. You won't shoot me; if you are brave you should tell the buck private to kill us with the monster he carries on his back. Let's hear you tell him if you're brave enough.

And I remember you, José, running behind the oxen along the road full of holes, the oxen that had escaped with the cart. I remember you running in your rubber boots, stepping aside while the oxen dashed forward, prodding them rapidly to get off the back road. The cart was coming down on top of you. You eluded it, and still holding the stick in your hand you kept after the oxen. And we screaming in the cart.

That was when we had a cart.

When we weren't so poor.

We had two oxen and a cow, but then bad times came and we decided to sell them and to buy with the money a sliver of land. You see, it's best to make the land produce, even if one had to use one's hands, that's what you used to tell me.

"The oxen and the cart are a luxury," I remember your words so clearly. No one bought the cart from us and it is rotting over there; at least it serves as a food stand. But with the sale of the oxen we were able to add to our little piece of land and to plant bananas; we also had more space for corn.

All right, I tell him, you know what you're doing. Because we were also getting rid of the cow that gave us milk that would be turned into cheese for the children. You'll see, things won't go badly for us.

And they haven't gone badly. We have food to eat and a spot to be buried in, at least. A few chickens that produce eggs for us and meat to sell. Back there we have planted some pineapples to be sold to Don Sebas. We have a good neighborhood. Everyone likes us because we have never done any harm to anyone. We are honorable unto death. The neighborhood knows that. Hard-working people. We live by the sweat of our brow. Everyone knows that. We have barely enough to get by, but we live. We don't wish anything bad to happen to anyone, not even now to Private Martínez.

The only thing we don't have is rights. And as we began to arrive at this awareness, this place filled up with authorities wishing to impose order, omnipotent, with their automatics as they call them. From time to time they come to see how we are behaving, who has to be taken away, who has to be beaten to be taught a lesson.

They want to force us with machetes and at gunpoint into resignation to our miseries. There is a kind of poverty they understand, the spiritual poverty they think they can force on us with their guns. And because they can't, they dream up their cruelties.

Luckily Adolfina didn't recognize him. Who knows what would have happened. Maybe they would have done away with us right then and there.

José was tough, he would have his few drinks and even shoot craps on Sundays. I used to tell him, stop gambling, it's dangerous, and after all, he had his bad habits from a certain point of view; but as soon as he began to speak up, becoming well-liked in the federation of farmworkers, everything changed for him.

Many years ago I would say to him: "You are a serious person, so why are you gambling; before you know it the Guard will show up and take you all away." And in self-defense he would say that he gambled for amusement, because in fact it was bad to shoot craps, but since there wasn't any other way to have fun around here, he had no alternative.

A little later, the young men and the priests came and formed the Federation of Christian Farmworkers, through which our requests for better loans have been channeled. And it has borne fruit; they have gotten a few little increases, and the men have become more serious since they now have something to believe in. The drinking even stopped, not to mention the crap shooting.

They began with some parties at the chapel; we would all make small contributions and buy chocolate and flour to make sweet bread and usually pineapple. And everyone had a great time. That was at the beginning.

Later on, there was no place for parties. Everyone wanted to devote their time to spreading awareness about the organization. Only once in a while is there a party, but above all it is to raise funds, or to help a neighbor in need, who is either out of a job or has lost a breadwinner. So, that's why we're having a better time of it. Why better if they beat us more than ever? Because now we know where we're headed. And they know that we know where we're headed. This explains the conduct of the authorities.

We don't brag about it. But we're getting there.

José Guardado accompanies us.

2:30 P. M.

I don't know how I managed to see that you were looking at me—your eye flicked open for only a moment, your only coffee-colored eye they had not touched. Maybe it was a sign, because it lasted barely a second. What an effort you must have made! Or maybe farewell. Or as they say: "Be careful not to give me away, be careful not to give yourself away or I will make you pay when these men release me." I didn't even vacillate. Once I made up my mind, my voice didn't quaver. Adolfina wasn't going to recognize you, the poor child didn't recognize you, which was much better for all of us: for Chepe, the children, Adolfina and me.

—Well, if you're sure you don't know him, we're going to parade him through the town. We're sure someone will identify him, because he smells like he's from this region.

—We are sure, as two and two makes four.

A guan bird has come to perch itself on the *tamarindo* branch. A beautiful guan bird with a fuzzy head and a long tail. It begins to flit around looking for dried *tamarindo* seeds to pick at.

I love birds, but José always refused to catch one for me: "Poor little things, why should we keep them locked up? They'll die of sadness." Birds can't withstand confinement. Even the mockingbird, which is perhaps the dearest and tamest bird, needs to be kept in the open. All you have to do is clip its wings and it will stay in the house; it's hopping around on the furniture. If you put it in a cage, it will stop singing. Who would want to remain confined, regardless of comforts? Let alone one accustomed to the air, the river and the trees.

—We will continue our search, maybe where they make tortillas.

—From house to house we are going to take him.

—It's because they have to go around redeeming that these things happen. Redeemers don't go over very well around here.

—Those who can't accept their fate.

—Maybe later they'll learn from the experience.

—Start the jeep.

And they leave, like hawks clutching between their claws the little children of the hens. With their claws they haul us, sure of themselves. To our eternal rest. For the second time you open the eye. It is not necessary for you to strain, it is not necessary for you to bid farewell; within a short time we will be seeing each other. Whichever of these days.

The odor of Chepe lingers, the same odor that he brings everyday from work, the clean and agreeable odor of the sweat of a real man. It is like the perfume of our life. One becomes accustomed to it and the pleasure is in conserving the moistness of the body. The body itself absorbs it. Maybe

199

deep within it nourishes us with this same sweat. At least
the men who sweat from sunset to sundown. Year after
year.

And I see like a trail in the sky, like the one that air-
planes leave when they pass overhead, a kind of smoke
that they expel from behind, they leave a palm leaf that
takes half a day to disappear. In the pristine sky, as if it
had just been bathed.

And I foresee the worst.

Now it will be up to me. To take care of the three little
children. I don't know whether there will be enough to
go around. This uncertainty is the worst—even with José
working we could barely afford beans. The beans we plant
are for the family use, but there is not enough to last all
year; more has to be bought sooner or later. Will we be
able to afford beans from just my work? That's what I
wonder.

Why is it that one thinks only about eating?

About food for the children. If we could just live on
air. Or maybe it's a profound sadness.

I foresee the worst. When death comes, it alerts you
before; it does not come all of a sudden. It always makes
a loud noise as if it were riding a horse galloping on a path
of stone, its hooves clattering on the stones, miserable
death. It makes fun of us because it knows we cannot re-
strain its runaway horses. It looks for us and finds us always
poor. There are problems in life. A child is sick, the beans
have burned. A son wounded or dead. We are always losing
in this game.

And now we must come from behind. We have a big
handicap difficult to discount. We are always like those

players who lose. And to think that we don't get tired. How much more blood will we lose?

We should not allow ourselves to get tired. For our children and for the children of our children. Someday the land will be ours and then we will begin to win. From behind. It's going to be difficult, Chepe. Don't think that bottles can be made only by blowing. Once we begin to win, they will not give us water. They will not forgive us; they will be implacable.

We are touching the balls of the tiger, and the tiger does not forgive. Now we have time only to think about our hardships, nothing more. Our mind has reached too far; they will not forgive us. Later we will see. For now, it is enough to think that it does not matter whether they forgive us. When all is said and done, we are in water up to our necks but we will not drown.

We will not drown in your absence, José. We will not drown.

Since the *chachalacas* appeared in the sky, I have not stopped thinking. The guans left but the *chachalacas* have come.

I remember when Adolfina was little, she didn't want to talk; she was two years old and could barely say papa and mama, dog, "tilla" for tortilla, "alt" for salt. And nothing more. We were very worried. María Pía told me that without doubt it was because they had a little parrot, maybe Adolfina used to eat the parrot's crumbs. Then the medicine man recommended that we give her *chachalaca* soup. I myself went to the doctor and he promised me that the *chachalacas* were going to make her talk. And that is what happened. We sometimes call *chachalacas* partridges. There they'd be all together in the morning among the pine trees making a lot of noise. Who can stop them? And who can shut them up? Already very early in the morning they are raising a ruckus. They go to get into the grass of the roof of the house. "Girl, go throw some stones at the *chachalacas*, don't let them wake up the baby because then I won't be able to do anything." And no matter how many stones one throws at them, they keep making their racket. The children went to sleep after eating, poor little things; they live tired and after the walk they took it was even worse.

Just five little soups of *chachalaca* drunk, and one day yes one day no—in a few days Adolfina was talking. That is why one should neither believe nor not believe. This is the key. There is the miracle.

Interminably they persist with their noise, over there among the pine trees, but one can be so contradictory! If they didn't come with their *chachalaca* talk, I would feel very sad. Lonely. The children are company, but because they're still little they don't mind playing by themselves, in silence. Only when they are sick do they cry. God has given me good children, I can't complain. Sick ones, that's true. Parasites eat them from the inside, and the children defend themselves by sleeping. Lucky that they have not been awakened. God is great.

Sweating, the afternoon walks across the clean sky.
Goodbye, José.

3 P.M.

José is very loving with the children, affectionate with all of them. When he comes back from the plantation, the first thing he does is ask about the children: if they have been crying a lot, if I have given them enough to eat. My heart goes out to him. He comes home all tired and sweaty, but even so he still finds time to play with them for a while or to take them for a walk nearby. In this matter I can't complain. He is a good father. You see, because they have so much work, men often don't spend much time with their children, as much as they would like. Go on, and he with so many things to attend to, especially in the cooperative, I wonder where he finds the time, the resilience he has. He amazes me, because other men are not as affectionate; it's not because they don't want to be but because they are always worrying about making ends meet. And only the women are responsible for taking care of the children.

You can't expect more from the men. From that point of view we peasant women are slaves, but it is not their fault. At bottom we help produce the wealth of the landowners when we take care of the children by ourselves, because we are also giving men the time to work in peace from sunup to sundown. That is to say, we are giving our time to the landowners so that our husbands can produce more, can be better exploited.

From that point of view we are also slaves, slaves obliged to clear the fields of the plantation, to pick the coffee on time and to make sure that the cotton is not messed up by the rains or by insects.

That is awareness, José would say. The soul also exists, he would tell me. It is of little importance to know where it is going. It is the soul of the people that lives here on earth.

—It looks to me that only you are killing yourself working.

—Your work is worse. Imagine having to stay home with the children all the blessed day, as a slave.

—Maybe when we work the *achiote*, it will be my turn.

Because our little plot does not sustain us, I started making *achiote*, at least during the season that it is produced, so as to sell it to Don Sebas. You see, people who travel on the paved road stop off to buy it. The *achiote* from around here is famous because it is nice and red and lasts a long time; it won't spoil, you know.

And finally. So many things come to you that just thinking about them is frightening. What will happen to José with only one eye? Because that eye he has already lost. Well, when we're born we're already half dead, but it is the other half that is important; this they can't control. It all depends on what we do with that half of life. Don't worry about me, José. I have not forgotten your words.

And he tells me: "These children must go to school."

—Yes, because it is a hard day's work.

—At least they should learn to read and write, that way they won't be so easily cheated.

—Well, that is what I'm telling you and that's why I have been thinking about buying a little fertilizer for the *achiote*, so we'll have a good crop and not have to depend only on the little they pay you at the plantation.

—And that way we won't send the children to work from the age of seven. It's better for them to go to school, even though I have to walk them there, it's so far away.

—It's what I'm saying, when there is a storm we won't send them because of the danger of the river flood.

—I'll help you in that business of the *achiote*.

And we were making a little something from the *achiote*, for many years. When the cooperative started, things changed a little, but as luck would have it, people don't want to use *achiote* in their food anymore. So now I don't kill myself nor do I stop producing, even if it's a little—whatever Don Sebas wants.

We're going to feel it deeply if something happens to him. We will bewail, we will try to be worthy of him so that he won't think that we are cowards and that we have forgotten everything we talked about.

—If anything happens to me, you know what to do.

—Hurry, I better knock on wood; you shouldn't think about such misfortunes. What you are doing is good . . .

—One never knows, Lupe.

—All right, I'm not incapable of taking care of things; should you disappear I would be able to look after myself.

—That's the way it is, don't go getting all upset. One should not be afraid of death, especially us. Death has become so familiar with us in these times, what with so many misfortunes our family has known, I wonder how we can withstand it because no matter how strong you are, you always get tired from the suffering of others.

I will miss you. "In any event, if something happens to me," José tells me, "don't worry. If the wild animals of the mountain eat me, don't grieve, because in any event, when one is dead one cannot feel anything, and it doesn't matter how one passes away." Imagine, he is always giving me courage! José is no innocent victim, he knows what he is doing. The poorer we become, the more we must struggle. All these things create the awareness that he talks about.

—You should see, Chepe, how you're convincing me that when you are dead you no longer feel anything . . .

—Of course, you feel nothing. It is like sleeping, and if before dying it is your lot to suffer a cruel death, it is all the same, because you have to make yourself believe that this pain will not follow you to the grave. The murderers who torture you are left with that pain.

—Hey, how you talk, and with everything that you tell me, I would like to die peacefully, as if I had fallen asleep, the way people used to die.

—You know how the authorities have gone around hassling people, how they have treated people we know, so it is best to assume that the same could happen to you.

—I'm not arguing with you . . .

—Well, of course, one would like to live better, to be better off and not have problems, but that is not fair. If we

don't put a little salt in our food, it will all be tasteless.
So it is best not to kill yourself trying to live . . .
—I say the same thing, even though it frightens me much,
and the truth is that when it's your turn, it's your turn.
What we don't know is how we will end up . . .
—Well, yes, we know how we were born but not how we
will die.

But don't think we talk about only sad things and
pessismism. He also tells stories.

And he has a way with stories. Just like my mother, he
gives a turn here and a twist there to what he's saying,
making you laugh, which is to say, they change the stories
around and invent things as they go along.

For example, my favorite is the one about the *Siguanaba*.
And you should hear it at night. There you are, trembling
from fright, thinking that the hairy hand is going to grab
you by the nipples. They say that the hairy hand has frozen
skin. But José says the hairy hand is just a hand with hair.
And I imagine it as a huge horse-biting spider walking
through the air. You have to wrap yourself up well in a
blanket, because if you don't, *mamita*, any movement will
have you imagining that it's the hairy hand.

He sits in the cart smoking his cigar and begins. Above
all he likes to tell stories when visitors are present, on full-
moon nights, when a few friends might arrive. And I with
my tobacco in my mouth, chewing, because I chew *magaya*,
listening to him just to be there next to the children so
they won't grow up nervous. Near them, hugging them.
"Don't be afraid, my son, that does not exist; they are only
stories." And how happy José gets at the center of a circle
of people listening to him. More than anything, I like it
when he spices up the stories, as in the case of the *Siguanaba*.

Well, it is true that around here a lot of people claim to have seen the *siguanaba*, either because she jumped out at them or because they saw her from a distance, but only Chepe knows how to tell the story with grace, without even scaring you. The whole world swears and insists that they have seen the *Siguanaba*. I believe only in their imagination.

But better not to keep on thinking because it can embitter one's life.

I knock on wood, yes indeed.

"You, too," I tell Adolfina. And she knocks on wood, even if she doesn't know why.

4 P.M.

A few days before, the authorities had arrived, but I didn't attribute much importance to it. Did José Guardado live there. I told Chepe, but I didn't tell him everything they said, so as not to worry him. I told them, "Yes, he lives here, what do you want?" "What does it matter to you? Our business is with him, not you, are you deaf?" All right, goodbye then, one can't even inquire about one's blood relations any longer; that's why I ask, of course it is important to me. They called me a meddlesome old woman, someone who is not satisfied with what God has given her. He won't be coming around here for a couple of weeks because he's down by the coast. He has been away a long time and it seems that he's forgotten us, that's what I told them.

—Fine, tell him that we're looking for him and that he had better be careful because we've found out a few things about him.

And there it ended; well, when he came home I told him,

and he answered that he had been working and that I could respond as God is our witness. "I have not been delinquent, let them come if they want; we have nothing to hide." And I got upset, I imagined them banging on the door, asking questions. They were intimidating us. Chepe, on the other hand, assumed indifference, perhaps to give me confidence.

And I remember that I told them that I had a lot of work, to please excuse me, as I wanted to bathe and couldn't do it with them there. I can't help you. And they tell me they're going to wait. I repeat, they can't wait because I won't be able to bathe because we don't have a bathroom. And they: "What a malicious old woman, and who is going to want to look at her, who is going to notice an old hag?" Until they got bored and left. More than a long hour, the Honduran kind; they were right there where they have been today. "We are coming back, we'll be back." Finally, they left.

They are courageous when it comes to abusing honorable people.

I wonder what they must be doing with you.

Where.

Who will recognize you, when they ask them who you are.

Who will say: "Chepe. It is Chepe Guardado." And he will come back here, defeated, and they are going to confront us. And what will happen to Adolfina and what will happen to my children? And what will happen to Chepe once they realize that he has lied to them?

Nothing will happen. That is what my heart tells me, no one from around here is going to tell them: "It is Chepe Guardado." No one. And the most horrible thing will happen. We are going to find him asleep somewhere, asleep in such a way as not to feel the animals picking at him nor the animals biting him: "Because when one is dead one does not feel anything."

Asleep forever stretched out on a pine trunk. Reclined. As if he were resting. And not even the ants will have touched him. And I will see him and not get perturbed because I am going to be ready to receive his dream.

His dream and my nightmare. And I am not going to cry, because his dream will be my hope. His words are reaching me already. "God is conscience. And conscience is we, the ones forgotten now, the poor."

And they will carry him to the mountain.

His companions will go look for him, with the animals in the air as their guide, the buzzards that fly in circles, gliding slowly, watching with their all-seeing eyes—over there, where the circles of the black birds are waiting, birds wanting to carry him off in their beaks.

And they won't find him.

Reclining on a pine tree. Feeling the cold mountain wind descending like a herd of goats from the pine forests of Honduras. And everyone will say here is Chepe, and I will arrive later because I will have fallen behind, covering myself with a shawl, because Holy Jesus it is so cold around here, my teeth chattering, my jaws shaking. I feel a chill all over my body. It is in these regions that flesh shivers. They have gone so far out of their way to dump him, climbing the cold windy mountains. The Honduran pine forests.

And they will find him with worms. Some worms eating Chepe. The body of Chepe. They will clean him then with the remains of a shirt. They will bathe him with water from the stream that flows from the mountain. They will envelop him in essence of mint. Because we go prepared for the worst. They will put fresh clothes on him: the nice little white shirt he wore on Sundays, the striped cotton pants he wore to go to chapel to talk with his companions. And they will say how emaciated the poor man has gotten in these past three days. Not having eaten, the poor man. And the dew he has endured. And the cold. Without his blanket. As if resting on the pine log.

And we will carry him back. They in front of me, because I don't have the strength to walk so much, and I am cautious about dry brush that might tear my dress. Dogs barking at us along the road. And we will go through the town and we will buy a box for him, an unpainted box. And we will go through town. People will say, "There they are, carrying Chepe." And I will still be shivering from the cold. Only my body, not my conscience.

All of this my heart told me. I don't know whether talk to me or to Adolfina. Conversing perhaps with the shadows.

And up to now my heart has never lied to me.

5 P.M.

Adolfina tells me it has been a rough day, but finally it's almost over.

And I start looking at the sun already sinking in the *guarumo* trees. "I wonder what has become of the gentleman," I tell her. She tells me: "What gentleman?" "The one they were carrying, the one with the eye gouged out. I am worried about what may happen to him." She tells me: "Don't think about it, Grandma, he will know what to do." I see tears coming to the eyes. The eyes of Adolfina are filled with tears. "Stop now," I tell her. "Forget it. Let's go have a little coffee. The children are playing in the corn bin; they must be hungry." "I've already had some, Grandma. I left yours over there." The children also ate; soon after the authorities left, I fed them. And I tell her: "Child, don't cry, what's the matter with you?" "Nothing, I'm thinking about María Romelia, about when we were on the Chalate bus, what would have become of me had they killed her?

Imagine, Grandma, where I met her, and I didn't even recognize her as someone I'd seen on my earlier visits here; the decisive way in which she carried herself, and to think she is just a child! Think of what she will be to us a few years from now!" And I tell her: "But, girl, I don't see any reason for crying; what is over is done with. And as for you, don't forget that you are just beginning to develop. María Romelia can't be more than two years older than you; what is happening to the world for you to speak to me like that, as if you were an old woman!" She responds:" My father helped me a lot, Grandma. Ever since I was a little child he has told me the origins of the injustices we suffer, the conscience that Grandpa Chepe talks about. What is happening to the world, Grandma, is that there is more than one María Romelia and we have yet to notice." I tell her: "All right, my love, leave things as they are; let's go inside because it is beginning to get damp and that can be bad for you; let's go see if the children who are being so quiet are out in the backyard. Get them for me, please, so they don't be bitten by insects." She wipes her face with her apron and we go in.

And she tells me: "Grandma, I wonder what has happened to my father, if they're going to bring him back to us or should we try to forget him." I am also thinking the same thing. "He helped me understand so many things about life. I am afraid of being on my own. You know my mother is another matter. My younger brothers consume all her time, she kills herself ironing for a living; her life is very domestic."

And I tell her: "You have me and your grandfather Chepe; you know that he also has his theories, and besides, he has earned a position as leader of the community. You can begin to imagine how much respect they have for him."

"You know something," she tells me. "You know something, Grandma: all of a sudden I saw the corpse of Private Martínez." I say: "Where, child?"

She tells me: "In my imagination, it came upon me like a revelation. His eyes and his mouth were open, and no matter how much they tried to shut his eyelids, they would open again, and no matter how much they pulled on his big toes, his mouth would not close. Standing around his body, his mother and his sisters were crying. And as they could not close his mouth, they put a lemon in it, so flies would not be able to get in, and so he wouldn't get wormy inside."

And I tell her: "Oh, child, that's a nightmare!" She tells me: "No, I think it's true, it has to be true."

I tell her: "But that's not possible, how could that be?"

She tells me: "My heart told me, and up to now my heart has never lied to me."

A shiver runs through my body as I light the candles.